Skipping Stones
at the CENTER of the
EARTH

Gemma,

I hope you enjoy my book, and I'll see you next year in the Middle School.

(Mr.) Andy Hueller

Andy Hueller

Bonneville Books
Springville, Utah

This is a work of fiction. The characters, names, incidents, places and dialogue are products of the author's imagination, and are not to be construed as real. The views expressed within are the sole responsibility of the author and do not necessarily reflect the position of Cedar Fort, Inc., or any other entity.

ISBN 13: 978-1-59955-488-4
Published by Bonneville Books, an imprint of Cedar Fort, Inc.
2373 W. 700 S., Springville, UT 84663
Distributed by Cedar Fort, Inc., www.cedarfort.com

LIBRARY OF CONGRESS CATALOGING-IN-PUBLICATION DATA

Hueller, Andy.
  Skipping stones at the center of the earth : a middle grade novel / Andy Hueller.
    p. cm.
  Summary: On a forgotten island at the center of the earth, twelve-year-old Cal Cobble lives at an orphanage evading a bully, avoiding all thought of the nearby prison, and dreaming of finding his father, until he meets the mysterious Mr. E and everything changes.
  Audience: 008-012.
  ISBN 978-1-59955-488-4
  [1. Conduct of life--Fiction. 2. Orphanages--Fiction. 3. Islands--Fiction. 4. Fathers and sons--Fiction. 5. Prisons--Fiction. 6. Schools--Fiction. 7. Bullies--Fiction. 8. Science fiction.] I. Title.

  PZ7.H8694Ski 2010
  [Fic]--dc22

                                          2010035561

Cover design by Angela D. Olsen
Cover design © 2011 by Lyle Mortimer
Edited and typeset by Megan E. Welton

Printed in the United States of America

10 9 8 7 6 5 4 3 2 1

Printed on acid-free paper

Praise for

Skipping Stones at the Center of the Earth

"Take a leap into a grand adventure! Hueller creates a world magical and mysterious; you will cheer (loudly!) for Calvin Comet Cobble on his unforgettable journey to take a courageous stand in a world that has come unscrewed."

—Kate St. Vincent Vogl, two-time honoree
in Lorian Hemingway's Short Story Competition
and author of *Lost & Found: A Memoir of Mothers*

"Take a little *Alice in Wonderland* fantasy, a sprinkling of *Holes'* reality, a dollop of mystery, and a dash of social commentary on the educational experience and you've got a great book! . . . There is plenty of suspense, mystery, and adventure as Cal and his friends Bernie and Mr. E find answers to their questions and discover some important truths about themselves in the process. This book was a page-turner from the first page to the last page, and I can easily see this book being made into a film. Highly Recommended!"

—Sandra McLeod Humphrey, winner of the Helen Keating Ott Award for Outstanding Contribution to Children's Literature and author of *Dare to Dream: 25 Extraordinary Lives.*

Also by Andy Hueller

*Dizzy Fantastic and Her
Flying Bicycle*

To my wife, of course;

To my parents, from whom I picked up the reading habit;

To my brother and sister, the first to see this story;

And to Matilda Wormwood, Charlie Bucket,

James Henry Trotter, Danny, and Sophie—

Calvin Comet Cobble's distant cousins and mentors

Bartholomew Rogers'

Three Important (and Simple!) Things to Remember for Antarctic Survival[1]

To Be Filled in as You Learn Them

1 _____

_____

_____

_____

2 _____

_____

_____

_____

3 _____

_____

_____

_____

1. From Rogers' international bestseller *How to Survive a Day at the Bottom of the World*.

To the Reader of This Story:

Twelve years ago, three men disappeared; one of these men is gone for good. Two years later, another man dropped from the face of the Earth. In four years, a young girl would vanish. A piece of hardware connects them all.

This book does not belong to any of these missing persons.

But their stories matter, patient reader.

They will matter to you (I hope). And they matter to a red-headed twelve-year-old boy—the boy to whom this book does belong.

Confused?

No matter. All will be set straight in good time.

Chapter 1

In the months following Bartholomew Rogers' discovery of a flathead screw with a head as big as Rhode Island underneath the snow and ice of Antarctica, elite geologists' conceptions of Earth were forever changed. Their models of the inside of our planet looked nothing like the ones scientists had studied for many decades previous. In the new models, the inside of the planet Earth was hollower, the mantle was thinner, and there was only one core, while in the old models, there had always been two (what were called the "inner" and "outer" cores). This core came to be known by scientists as "The Pit of the Planet" because, as a solid sphere right in the middle of Earth, it more closely resembled the pit of a peach than it did the core of an apple.

Globes and maps of Earth were forever changed, too. Not long after Mr. Rogers discovered his screw, America discovered and adopted its newest major city: "Robert."

The city is an island, surrounded by miles and miles of ocean, though it technically belongs to the state of Alaska.

Perhaps you already know all about Robert, Alaska. Maybe your parents work in some super-secret capacity and have witnessed important decisions being made. I suspect not, however. Less than a thousand people on Earth know anything about Robert. Have you been asked to identify the city on a school geography test? If a classmate nudged a globe your way, could you find Robert, Alaska, population: 521? How about your teacher? Will your teacher show you Robert on a map of the world?

I didn't think so.

How, reader, would you like to live in a place so utterly forgotten nobody can find it? How would you like to be one of 521 misplaced Americans—dropped like change under couch cushions and never thought of again?

This is the story of Cal Cobble. He lives in Robert, Alaska—America's forgotten city. This is the story of one of the forgotten 521.

Chapter 2

Seven Years Ago
(Five Years After Unscrewing Bart's Screw)

It had rained the night before, and the morning air was still damp and cool as Calvin Comet Cobble sat on the curb in front of the Detroit orphanage he was leaving. Despite the goose bumps prickling up and down his arms, legs, and neck, all of his attention now was on a small, pink earthworm. Cal had spotted the earthworm as it made its way to the middle of the busy street, and he had watched its glacial progress for more than an hour. When a car zoomed by, Cal turned away and cringed, assuming the earthworm was done for—and yet each tire missed it. Invariably, the small, pink earthworm was in the right place at the right time. As it moved closer to its goal, Cal cheered for it. He forgot about the mysterious place to which they were sending him. (Where on Earth was it, anyway?) All he cared about that afternoon was the earthworm making it to the other curb unscathed.

Cal stood up—for the eleventh time that morning—and

stepped into the street after the earthworm, but traffic was too busy and constant, and he didn't make it three steps away from the road's shoulder before a car rushed by him, so close and so loud he first felt the tip of his nose with his fingertips to see if he still had it, and then he wondered if he'd permanently lost some hearing. He whistled a note and clucked his tongue. He could hear both sounds. He seemed okay. Alas, the earthworm had to fend for itself.

Cal could empathize. He was five years old, the orphanage in Detroit was all he'd ever known, and today he would travel to a new home—"a longer-term solution," he'd been told. He had no idea where he was going, though. To make things worse, it was out of his control. The biggest decision of his young life, and he didn't have a choice. The Question burst into his mind then, as it often did: Where was his dad? He knew his mother had died bringing him to the world, but no one ever could (or would?) tell him anything about his father. Whenever he asked an adult at the orphanage about his dad, they immediately changed the subject. Cal forced the Question from his mind. He knew there was nothing he could do, no way to find an answer. No, Cal didn't want to think of his dad or his mysterious new life right then. He just wanted the earthworm to make it across the street.

The closer the earthworm got—millimeter by painfully slow millimeter—the more it meant to Cal. Cal lay down on his stomach and watched the earthworm make its progress under roaring, speeding cars and trucks. Its progress so gradual Cal thought at times that it wasn't moving forward at all. It was impossible that the earthworm would make it across the street, Cal knew. *But he's made it this far,* he reminded himself. *He has. He has.*

When the earthworm was only two feet and probably seven minutes from the other curb, a blue Taurus appeared in front of Cal. A man wearing a flannel shirt and a baseball cap got out of the passenger seat and opened the back door. "This is your ride, Calvin Comet Cobble," the man said.

The Taurus' interior was foggy with cigarette smoke, and the seat belts in back smelled like someone's armpit. Cal didn't complain, though. He knew it wouldn't do any good. He didn't get a vote. He never had a choice.

It was out of his control.

The blue Taurus merged back into the highway traffic. Cal would never know if the earthworm made it.

Chapter 3

It was a sunny 71 degrees Fahrenheit in Robert. Cal and the rest of the Hidden Shores orphans were playing Hide and Go Seek. The orphans often played Hide and Go Seek, though it was, by almost any line of reasoning, an odd choice of game.

At Hidden Shores, there just aren't many places to hide. Sneaking, running, and certainly hiding are strictly prohibited in the building itself, and outside there's only a long, wide front lawn with one maple tree between the orphanage and the rock beach a couple hundred yards away. There is a shack up there on the rock beach, a small falling-apart wood abode—but that's where Mr. E lives, and the orphans certainly aren't going to ask him if they can hide in his house.

When playing Hide and Go Seek, some of Hidden Shores' orphans climbed into the maple tree's branches. They all called her Roberta or, affectionately, Aunt

Robbie. A brave orphan would follow the seeker around, staying just behind him, hoping not to be discovered too early in the game. Most orphans pressed their backs to the orphanage or their chests to the grass and kept quiet.

Cal, six years old now, wondered why this was the game they chose to play. They didn't have any playground equipment, he recognized—no tetherball poles, no balls of any kind, no slides or swings or teeter-totters. All of these things cost money, and Principal Warden wasn't about to spend it. So maybe it made sense after all, Cal thought, that the orphans played the game Hide and Go Seek. They all knew it from before they came to Robert. One day they started playing, and everyone knew the rules, and despite the brevity and futility of each round, they just kept on playing, day after day. Cal thought maybe Hidden Shores orphans didn't mind being spotted. No one ever seemed too disappointed when the seeker said, "I see you!" When you lived in an orphanage in the center of the planet, on America's least-often visited island, it felt good to be found, even if it was just a game.

Maybe the game, Cal thought, *should be called Hide and Get Found. And if getting found is the goal, I guess I'm really good at this game.*

Cal tended to be the first orphan spotted.

It was all because of his hair.

Cal had the brightest and wildest shock of messy, red-orange hair any kid in Robert had ever seen. No matter how much water or hairspray or gel he drenched it with, his hair was always heading in a thousand directions.

He'd lived in Robert for only three weeks when Hidden Shores orphans and teachers decided that Cal's head looked like it was on fire. The orange freckles that dotted his face, they agreed, resembled smoldering embers. Sometimes when the seeker found Cal, he said, "I'm putting out a grassfire!" or "Someone call the fire department!" They all laughed at him then. "There is no fire department," Cal would mutter to himself. "There's just this school and that prison over in the Shadow—"

That's when Cal would shiver and quit his muttering. He didn't want to talk—not even to himself—about what lurked in the looming darkness to his left.

Truth be told, there is one good hiding spot in Robert, Alaska. No—it's not just good. It's the best hiding spot in the world, and that's a fact.

Robert is The Pit of the Planet, the very center of planet Earth—sometimes called "Bob" by Robertians because Bob is short for Robert. (The name fits, also, because the island-city floats like a fisherman's enormous bobber in a great saltwater lake that used to be half of the Arctic Ocean.)

Robert is named after the author Robert Louis Stevenson, who wrote a book, *The Strange Case of Dr. Jekyll and Mr. Hyde*, about a character with two different personalities. If ever a city had two distinct personalities, Robert is that city. The right side of the island is lit by the sun during the day and populated by wide-eyed, generally innocent but down-on-their-luck children who live in a tall, cereal box–shaped red brick orphanage. The left side is enveloped by a great and unrelenting Shadow hiding a prison full of dangerous, murderous criminals.

The orphans of Robert have nowhere else to live. They're the unwanted orphans, the ones nobody adopted when they lived in other places. They come from all over the United States. They are poor, parentless, and young. The oldest orphan in Robert is fourteen. The youngest is five. They were all sent to the orphanage in Robert because they needed a home. Everyone needs a home, after all.

The right side of the island gets its sunlight from a hole dug in northeastern Alaska. That means only one half of the island is illuminated, and only during the day. That's where Hidden Shores Orphanage resides—in the sunlight. The other half of the island, the Shadow, has never seen sunlight. In the Shadow crouches Robert Inner-planet Penitentiary, home of the world's nastiest, beastliest criminals. They are serial killers, endangered animal hunters, or kidnappers. They get a thrill out of bringing harm to the innocent. These criminals were sent to Robert so they'd be far away from Earth's citizens. In Robert's great Shadow, these criminals sit and wait. They plan the heinous crimes they'll commit when they escape. When an orphan misbehaves or speaks out of turn, a teacher will say, "How about spending next period alone in the Shadow?" That orphan's eyes go wide and she cooperates, no questions asked.

If anyone were to step into the Shadow, Cal and every other orphan knew, they'd win that round of Hide and

Go Seek. No one would look for them there. No one would follow them in.

This morning, the thought of it—of being alone in the Shadow, the world's darkest and scariest place—quickened Cal's breathing. And then he couldn't help himself. He did what he promised himself he wouldn't do. He glanced up at it—at the pure, unrelenting darkness. Now he could hear and feel his heartbeat. Everything else went silent. All that existed were his heartbeat and the Shadow's silent groan. (*How peculiar*, Cal thought. *The Shadow's so quiet it's like I can hear its silence.*) The Shadow seemed to move closer every time he looked at it. The seeker, behind him, finished counting aloud the forty seconds the hiders had to hide. "Thirty-two Hidden Shores . . . Thirty-three Hidden Shores. . . ." Cal caught a glimpse of a classmate, Belinda Poof, on the sun-sparkled green grass in front of him. She was standing, her head swiveling like an owl's as she frantically looked for a place to hide. *I guess she'll be the first one the seeker finds*, Cal thought.

"Thirty-six Hidden Shores," the seeker, an older orphan named Kyle Nordstrom, said behind him. "Thirty-seven Hidden Shores."

Cal watched Belinda and felt bad for her. As vulnerable as Cal was with his flaming red hair, he at least wasn't standing up in the middle of the lawn. He wanted to say, "Get down, Belinda! Do something!" He wanted to say this until he saw what she planned to do.

"Thirty-nine Hidden Shores . . ."

That's when Belinda took off. In the wrong direction.

She ran toward the Shadow.

Cal couldn't believe it. "No—Belinda!" he shouted. Except he didn't shout it. He meant to, he really did. In his head, it was a shout. Out loud, however, it was hardly a whisper.

Belinda took one final stride, half her leg disappeared, and then—Poof!—she was gone.

Cal stood. Stunned.

"Ready or not, here I come," Kyle announced. "Ha ha! Cobble—I see you. You look like human candle. Ever thought about hiding?"

Cal turned to Kyle. "She ran in there." He pointed to the darkness.

"What are you talking about, Cobble? Who ran in there."

"She did. B-Belinda. She—she ran in there."

Kyle's eyes got big. "In there?" He smirked. "You're lying to me. I'm not falling for it, Cobble."

"No—she's in there!" Now he really was shouting.

Heads rose all around them—the hiders getting up off of their stomachs and standing. The orphans could hear the honesty in Cal's voice.

One of them walked until she was twenty feet from the Shadow, as close as any orphan ever got. She shouted, "Belinda! Belinda! Come out!"

And then the rest of them joined in, all shouting "Belinda!" at the same time.

Mr. Bruno, the physical education teacher, who spent all day sitting on the orphanage's front steps, looked up from his Louis L'Amour book, finished rolling his smoke, and moseyed over to join the group of orphans. He walked right up next to the Shadow and said, "Poof? Poof? You in there?"

When she didn't respond, Mr. Bruno took off his Brooklyn Dodgers baseball cap with the dusty brim, ran his hands through his hair and then down his unshaven face. He stood there, his head in his hands, for a long moment. Nobody moved. And then he took out a match, struck it against his jeans, and lit his hand-rolled cigarette. He blew two streams of smoke through his nostrils into the Shadow.

When Mr. Bruno turned around, his eyes were wet. He moseyed back to the front steps, opened his book, and resumed reading.

Belinda Poof, they all knew, was gone.

The first girl who'd called for her, Meredith, stormed toward Cal. "You! You little red-haired nincompoop. What's wrong with you? You let her go in there? Why didn't you yell for help? Why didn't you tell her to stop?" She hit Cal in the chest with the bottom of her fist and then with the bottom of the other one. As she pounded Cal, she cried. "You idiot! You idiot! You idiot!"

Cal took the pounding. It was out of his control.

Chapter 4

This Very Year
(Twelve Years After Unscrewing Bart's Screw)

Cal Cobble, now twelve years old, slipped out of bed and tiptoed out of his room on the ninth floor of Hidden Shores Orphanage and into the long narrow hallway. Cal wore a faded green T-shirt and blue denim shorts—more like capris—that used to be pants. The hallway's wood floor had a tendency to creak, so Cal took his time. Stretching each step farther than the last, he touched the floor with the big toe of his right foot first, as though testing the temperature of pool water from the deck, before easing down onto his heel and then sliding his left foot up to his right. Despite Cal's precautionary methods, the floor creaked and moaned. He winced each time the rickety wood complained. If anyone heard him he'd be in trouble.

Big trouble.

Teachers were always trying to catch Cal causing trouble. He had a reputation for being wild, uncontrollable—a real rabble-rouser.

It was his hair that did it. People all over and inside this world are, by nature, reluctant to trust a child with wild red hair.

Hector Nelson, the orphanage's most feared fourteen-year-old bully—who claimed his dad was an inmate at Robert Inner-planet Penitentiary—called Cal "Torch." Hector had been held back three grades and sat behind Cal in Miss Trudy's seventh-grade classroom. He picked on all the kids, but Cal was his favorite target. One time, Hector even set Cal's hair on fire with his cigarette lighter.

Half of Cal's hair had been singed before Berneatha Twiggins, the seven-year-old, pig-tailed girl smart enough to be in a seventh-grade class, and Cal's only real friend inside or outside the planet, threw her shoe at the glass case that held the fire extinguisher at the front of the room, dropping the extinguisher with a clang to the floor. She'd scrambled to the front of the classroom, grabbed the fire extinguisher, scurried back to Cal's desk, and saved the rest of his hair.

"I was just trying to make the fire on his head more real-like," Hector explained to the principal, after having his recess privileges revoked for two weeks. Of course, Cal's recess privileges had been revoked, too, for provoking Hector.

"Control that hair of yours, Mr. Cobble," Principal Warden said. "I cannot in good conscience blame Mr. Nelson alone. How is a boy with a healthy temper like his to control himself with your red hair blazing away in his face? And I refuse to believe that any boy with a father like yours would ever be entirely innocent in a problem situation such as this."

All the hair from the back of his head down to the nape of his neck in flames only minutes before, Cal was too stunned to defend himself or ask what Principal Warden meant about his father. He had overheard teachers at the orphanage talking about "the father of that red-headed boy Miss Trudy says is so much trouble." He never knew what they meant. He never asked them, though. He knew they wouldn't tell him anything. So he let it be.

It was out of his control.

When Cal's hair grew back, it was somehow even wilder than before. It was as if his hair had taken offense to being set on fire. Before encountering Hector's lighter, Cal's hair had been stubbornly messy; now it was angrily messy, refusing to straighten even for a moment, even when wet.

Now, sneaking out of the orphanage, Cal didn't want any trouble, for himself or anyone else. He wanted to be alone. To forget about his life—his parentless, virtually friendless life—at Hidden Shores Orphanage. And the best part of being up so early was that nearly everyone else in Robert was sleeping. He'd slipped out of bed and snuck out of the orphanage the past sixty-three mornings, and every morning, for about an hour, it felt to Cal like the island was his. Or at least half his, anyway.

Cal inched past two fire poles.

* * *

There are no staircases inside Hidden Shores Orphanage. Six fire poles run through the floors as straight and evenly distanced as guitar strings.

If you've ever been to a fire station or seen a movie about firefighters, you know that there are holes in the upper floors of a fire station, and that poles run from the bottom level of the fire station up through these holes in the floors to the ceiling. Firefighters grab hold of the poles and slide down them to their fire trucks on the bottom floor and then race away to douse burning buildings, rescue people in danger, and recover cats run up a tree by the neighbor's dog.

The fire poles at Hidden Shores are just like the fire poles at any fire station. When an orphan at Hidden Shores looks down or up a fire pole hole, she can see down to the cafeteria on the bottom floor and up to the ceiling above the tenth floor.

The bedrooms and classrooms for the youngest orphans, the kindergartners, are on the second floor, and the orphans who are slightly older than the youngest sleep and go to class on the third floor, and those who are slightly older than the second youngest do these things on the fourth floor, and so on and so forth all the way up to the tenth floor, where the oldest orphans at Hidden Shores, the eighth-graders, sleep and go to class. There are fifteen girls and fifteen boys in each grade. The fifteen boys share one bedroom and the fifteen girls another. By the time orphans are old enough to live on one of the top floors, they've become very adept at sliding down fire poles. And, though it isn't as glamorous, they've also become very adept at shinnying up fire poles. There are three poles designated as "down" poles, and three others as "up" poles. They alternate. Next to every "down" pole is an "up" pole, and next to every "up" pole is a "down" pole.

A person might think, *That sounds like fun! I'd like to slide down a fire pole.* But the fire poles at Hidden Shores Orphanage aren't there for the orphans' amusement. If you visited the orphanage—something you are of course not permitted to do under any circumstances—you would never glimpse the orphans racing up and down the poles. You wouldn't hear them shriek or whoop as they slide down, either. Principal Warden maintains that a quiet school is a successful school. That means voices must be kept down in the classrooms, in the cafeteria, outside at recess, and on the fire poles. Hidden Shores Orphanage installed fire poles in place of a staircase because they're inexpensive and easy to keep up. You don't have to spend any money or do any maintenance on a fire pole. If the pole's stable, gravity takes care of the rest. (Once a week, as the orphans perform their chores, six orphans from the tenth floor clean the poles. One orphan wraps a towel wet with sanitizing oil around each pole and then clasps the towel around the pole while sliding down to the cafeteria on the ground floor.)

There are occasional accidents. An orphan in his first week or two at Hidden Shores will walk to an "up" pole when she intends to go down. She will compound her mistake and forget to check that the pole is clear before sliding down. The new orphan won't see, then, that another orphan is shinnying up the pole at that same moment. These accidents always end with broken bones. One of the accidents, years ago, ended with fatalities. Such mistakes are undoubtedly tragic but quite infrequent. Hidden Shores orphans use the poles several times a day, and they seldom forget which poles are intended for sliding and which ones for shinnying. They rarely forget to, as they say, "look both ways."

A shuddering, puttering elevator runs from the tenth floor at Hidden Shores Orphanage down to the first floor, and from the first floor up to the tenth. Only teachers are permitted to use it. One teacher lives on each floor of the orphanage, in his or her own room, the next door over from the classroom at the end of the hall. While the teaching salary at the school in Robert doesn't compare to that at an American school on the outside of the world, teachers boast that they do get room and board.

Except, that is, for Mr. Bruno, the phys ed teacher. He sleeps in a small canvas tent behind the orphanage and cooks his own meals over a small fire he builds and extinguishes each day.

* * *

The flames on top of Cal's head were especially unruly after a night of being slept on. Tufts of hair from the front of his head pointed up and back while tufts from the back of his head pointed to the ceiling and to his left ear. At the moment, though, lying on his stomach and peeking down a hole in the ninth floor to make sure nobody was milling around on the first floor, Cal wasn't concerned about his hair. His focus now was not getting caught out of bed. Convinced he was the only orphan or teacher awake, he got to his feet, grabbed the fire pole in front of him, and jumped. He wrapped his legs around the pole as he began to slide.

Cal held back a chirp of glee as he zoomed downward.

In four and a half seconds, he was down the pole and standing in the empty cafeteria on the bottom floor. He heard the cooks in the kitchen to his left as they prepared breakfast for two-hundred and seventy orphans. Mr. and Mrs. Grossetta sung along off-key to some folk song playing low on a boombox. Cal shuffled across the tile floor to the oak front door, turned the brass lock and then the knob, and slowly, carefully, pushed it open. He stepped outside and closed the door behind him—slowly, carefully, ever-so-softly. Then he scampered to the maple tree twenty yards away.

"Here I come, Aunt Robbie," Cal said under his breath, mid-scamper.

For over two months now, Cal had been sneaking silently out of the orphanage every morning before breakfast. He'd spent every one of those mornings sitting on his favorite of Roberta the maple tree's limbs.

The grand tree stood thirty feet tall, and, because the sun always came from the same place, she angled up toward it at about forty-five degrees. Using Roberta's branches for handholds, Cal walked right up her trunk. Twelve giant steps up the trunk and Cal, even with his blazing red hair, was lost to the world, hidden behind thousands of green leaves.

Cal sat on his branch and waited. He felt the deep Shadow to his left—the awful prison and the violent prisoners—without looking at it. Cal kept his eyes on the still water of Lake Arctic. The sun crept into the hole in the horizon, lighting half the island and painting a sparkling trail all the way across Lake Arctic to the shores of Bob. This trail of sunlight came each morning, and it always looked solid and inviting to Cal. He'd often felt the urge to run on top of it all the way to the other side of the lake, to Earth's Mantle, so very far away, dark as your night sky—cracked with orange lava oozing between tectonic plates. Cal knew that the Mantle, the outside of which served as Earth's crust, was the barrier between the Alaskan city of Robert and the normal world. The world where adults buy and sell and solve and cure and whatever else they do to make money. Where kids go to school during the day and then go home to have dinner with their parents and siblings. Where people experience more than a few hours' direct sunlight each day. Where—yes, way up there, through that hole, and then in any direction you headed—people are generally happy, even if they are in some other orphanage, as Cal had been before they brought him to this terrible and forgotten place. He'd never been out to the Mantle (or even to the water, as certified lifeguards cost money Principal Warden said

Hidden Shores simply didn't have), but he imagined it felt like warm coffee grounds spread over drying cement.

Cal chewed on these thoughts as he waited on his favorite of Aunt Robbie's limbs.

At long last, Mr. E showed up, right on time.

Chapter 5

Mr. E mowed Hidden Shores Orphanage's vast green front lawn. Seven afternoons a week, fifty-two weeks a year, he hopped on his riding lawn mower and drove back and forth, back and forth, for four and a half hours, keeping the grass short but (with the help of an electric sprinkler system that rose from the grass in the evenings) soft and forever green. The four and a half hours he mowed the lawn every afternoon was the only time anybody ever saw Mr. E.

Anybody but Cal, that is.

For sixty-three mornings, Cal had watched Mr. E emerge from his wooden shack near the shoreline and walk barefooted across the rock beach about two hundred yards from the front door of Hidden Shores Orphanage. His gait was long and easy, and, as he strode along, he leaned forward and looked down at the ground with the concentration of an early bird looking for breakfast worms. He glided over the rocks, like he was walking over a patch of the grass he maintained and not pointy purplish stones. His feet, Cal thought, must be tough— callused from walking on the rocks every day.

Mr. E was probably seven feet tall, but his shack was hardly bigger than a doghouse. Cal had always been amazed that anyone could live there. He didn't think a full-size single mattress would even fit inside. He imagined Mr. E folding himself up like an origami toy in order to sleep each night.

Mr. E was the only citizen of Robert not associated with either the orphanage or the prison. He was the one in the city's official population of five hundred and twenty-one. Two hundred thirty-seven citizens at the prison in the Shadow: two hundred of them prisoners plus thirty-five guards, a cook, and a warden. Two hundred eighty-three at the orphanage in the sunlight: two hundred and seventy of them orphans, ten teachers, two cooks, and a principal. And then there was Mr. E, right up against the shoreline, as close to the Shadow as you could get without vanishing.

Of course, Mr. E was not his official name. If you were to find his birth certificate, you'd know that his last name was more than the fifth letter of the alphabet. But none of the orphans knew Mr. E's real name. Nobody even remembered who first called the man in the shack Mr. E, but whomever or wherever the name had come from, it had stuck. No Hidden Shores orphan ever dared talk or make eye contact with Mr. E, not when he was mowing the lawn and certainly not when he was in his shack.

From his leafy hideout, Cal watched Mr. E pace back and forth along the rock beach. He was bald and dark-skinned and wore the same thing every morning: a gray-striped white dress shirt clumsily tucked into black dress pants, the sleeves rolled up almost to his elbows; and, around his neck, a purple tie—on backward, so it swung behind him when he walked. His bald head shone under the sun. Though everybody called him Mr. E, he didn't look much older than twenty or, at the most, thirty. Sometimes it was hard to tell. Cal figured the orphans called him Mister because he was older than they were and because he owned his own house, however small it was.

The orphans were always making fun of Mr. E, calling him "crazy," "nutty," "kooky," and just about any other adjective you can think of that's somewhat synonymous with "mentally unsteady." They made fun of him, laughing nervously, because they were afraid of him and didn't want to admit it. They really wanted to call him "creepy," "scary," or any other adjective somewhat synonymous with "he makes me shiver and want to hide under the bed." They asked themselves, *Why would anyone choose to live here? Who is he hiding from? Who is he being kept away from? Why does he like mowing the lawn so much?*

But Cal knew something about Mr. E none of the other orphans knew: Mr. E was probably the greatest skipper of rocks who ever lived.

As Mr. E walked the rock beach, his left arm swung loose at his side, like it didn't have any muscle or bone. His right arm, besides being very, very long and very, very slender, looked just about like everyone else's. But his left arm, his stone-skipping arm, was special. It looked an awful lot like a rope, Cal thought, just swinging freely at Mr. E's side.

Cal was at this moment—as he was at every moment of every day—aware of the Shadow looming menacingly to his left. And he knew, even at this moment, that somewhere out there in the darkness was a prison, a building crammed full of vicious, violent men. No Hidden Shores orphan ever forgot about Robert Inner-planet Penitentiary (R.I.P.). But when he watched mysterious Mr. E skip stones, Cal was less aware of the dangers to his left. He was able, at least, to pretend to forget about the serial killers, endangered animal hunters, and kidnappers (and those who were all three) who, he knew, were plotting to torture and kill him that very moment.

And so Cal watched Mr. E, feeling alone and free and, as much as possible, safe. His stomach stiffened in anticipation.

Cal marveled at the way his enigmatic neighbor could make a rock bounce on water. Even watching him prepare to skip stones was exciting. Mr. E's preparation was elaborate, perfected.

As he paced the rock beach now, Mr. E's chin seemed glued to his chest. His eyes never left the rocks below him. He paced the beach for fifteen minutes, frequently bending to pick up a stone. Usually, Mr. E dropped the stone right back where he found it. Occasionally, he kept it, closing the fingers of his right hand around it.

Cal had come to understand that only certain rocks were worthy of being skipped and most were not. He didn't know what made a rock worthy of such an honor. He was too far away to see what kind of rocks Mr. E kept.

After he'd collected five rocks, Mr. E stood up straight and walked to the water's edge. He turned sideways, so he was facing his shack ninety feet away. He widened his stance and bent his knees.

Cal's breath caught for a second. Mr. E was about to skip his first stone of the morning.

Bent over like a pitcher getting his sign from the stretch, Mr. E held his stone between the pointer finger and thumb of his left hand, about knee high. His rope of a left arm swayed gently at his side. And then it started to move. It swung back and up like a tree swing. His arm was free of tension as it swung, and it tugged his hand—holding the stone—like a rope tugs a rubber tire and a smiling child. The tie he had on backwards swung, too, in the opposite direction of his arm. When his hand and tie were about as high as his ears, they hesitated. They stopped just for a moment.

Cal knew most people probably wouldn't notice Mr. E's arm stop. He could see it stop only because he'd been watching Mr. E skip stones for the past sixty-three mornings.

Then Mr. E's arm swung down toward the water: the

tree swing falling forward.

He pushed off his long, thin, bent back leg.

His shoulders and hips turned so he faced the water.

When his hand was back where it started, only as high as his knee, he flicked his wrist and released the stone. If Mr. E's left arm were a tree swing, the rubber tire had ripped loose from the rope and was now soaring away fast.

His arm finished its parabolic motion without the rock. His left hand ended up near his right ear.

Cal watched as Mr. E's stone hovered just over the water of Lake Arctic for what must have been hundreds of yards (the length of at least three football fields) like it didn't want to drop, like it couldn't swim and was afraid of the water.

Finally, forty-five or fifty seconds after the stone had left Mr. E's hand, it touched down on the still, waveless water, skimmed the surface, and bounded forward. And then it touched down and bounded forward again. And again it touched down and bounded forward. And again. And again. And again. And again. The rock left rings that expanded in the water as it went.

Cal listened to the rock bounce. Soon he couldn't see it anymore, but he could hear it. Each time it touched the water it made a softer sound.

Ta . . . . . ta . . . . ta . . . ta and on and on and on, the sounds getting closer together but softer and softer until he couldn't hear them at all.

Mr. E lay down on his stomach, moved his ear over

the edge of the water, and listened. He could still hear it, Cal knew.

Cal waited and watched and listened.

What must have been twelve minutes later, Cal heard the rock again.

Thwack.

Sploosh.

The stone had hit the Mantle and then dropped into the water. Because there is no wind, sound travels a long way inside Earth. And the stone hitting the Mantle and falling back to the water made enough noise to be heard all the way back on the shores of Robert, if you listened carefully.

Cal always listened carefully. Now, sitting in Aunt Robbie's boughs, he grinned.

The stone had skipped clear across Lake Arctic.

Mr. E stood up, dug his feet in, and threw another.

Chapter 6

Fifteen Years Ago

"What do we have here?"

That's what explorer Bartholomew Rogers might have thought, if he gave himself time to think. If he ever again gave himself time to think.

He was on his knees, digging with his lime-green mittens into the Antarctic snow beneath him. Lime-green was his favorite color. His thick rubber boots, his puffy nylon snowsuit, the goggles he wore to protect his eyes from the cold, all the way up to his stocking cap—all of it was lime-green.

His bushy brown beard wasn't lime-green, of course, but it wasn't brown at the moment, either. And for that matter, it wasn't bushy. Buried under a layer of snow and ice, Bartholomew's beard was currently as white as a wizard's. There he was, sweating despite the dangerous cold, his mind busier than an Internet search engine, his knees sore from kneeling, in such a hurry he was throwing whole handfuls of snow behind him, over his shoulders, and at the bottom half of his face. If he stood up, Bartholomew would have looked like a Popsicle frosted with freezer burn.

And then, as abruptly as he'd started digging, he stopped.

He pushed his goggles to his forehead to get a better look. There was a sparkle in each of his eyes. His wind-burned lips worked their way into the beginnings of a grin. He'd been exploring Antarctica for two years now, and finally, after measuring and weighing and examining snow for so long it was no longer for him just frozen stuff you sled on and compact into balls to throw at your buddies—after all this time, he finally might have found something interesting. Thirty-three years of age, carrying a few too many pounds, alone in the loneliest and coldest place on Earth, Bartholomew Rogers suddenly and without warning felt something he hadn't felt for a very, very long time—never once in the adult life he'd dedicated to locating and understanding distant destinations. The sensation rushed through his body like warm blood.

That old boyhood triumph: discovery.

* * *

Back when his classmates were decorating their bedroom walls and ceilings with posters of sports teams and movie stars and rock bands, Bartholomew had covered his with atlases and photographs of far-away places he'd ripped from the issues of *National Geographic* piled sloppily all around the room. Before falling asleep at night, when Bartholomew was a boy, he would lie on his bed in the middle of his bedroom and stare up at the ceiling, his mind inevitably wandering from the photographs to the atlases: puzzles they were, the pieces all colors and shapes and sizes, representing every known place on the planet Earth. Each one just a few short steps and a leap of the imagination away. There was the interactive thrill of pushing a red wall tack into a tiny or unpopulated puzzle piece and announcing to the world, "This is where I'm going to go."

* * *

Now, grown up and paddling snow off of something hard and shiny that may have been—was it? Could it be?—gold, Bartholomew could see himself inside those maps. He would be the red tack. He would spend a couple years camping in the Sahara Desert, Bartholomew thought. And then perhaps a few years breathing the deliciously oxygen-thin air at the peak of a Himalayan mountain. Images of the uninviting places that had always seemed so inviting to Bartholomew flickered like a slideshow in his brain, no one slide illuminated for more than a moment. He was too excited to collect his thoughts. He drooled as he fantasized about the adventures he'd take if what he'd found was, indeed, gold.

The drool froze to his chin.

But even Bartholomew Rogers—who'd spent a life-time desiring nothing but to explore the remotest of the remote places of the planet Earth—could not possibly imagine how far into the uncharted world his discovery would take him.

* * *

After seven hours of digging, Bartholomew had uncovered a tennis court-size slab of what he thought was gold. The sun reflected off of it and made him squint.

* * *

After a week of digging with a spruce-handled, steel-headed shovel he retrieved from his canvas tent, he'd uncovered a slab the size of several soccer fields.

He kept digging.

* * *

Day after day he found more gleaming metal.

With pliers, Bartholomew yanked a gold-capped molar from his mouth and compared it to the hard, shiny metal he'd spent weeks uncovering.

He was now certain he'd found gold.

* * *

After a year and seven months of digging all day and sleeping only four hours a night, Bartholomew thought he'd finally reached the end of the gold. When he drove his shovel down to the ground, the edge of the blade broke the surface of the South Pole snow. When he drove it down again, the blade sunk a quarter of an inch deeper.

It felt odd not to hit metal, actually. By then he'd grown accustomed to hearing the sweet ping produced each time the steel blade met gold an inch or two beneath the snow's surface.

Bartholomew packed three Ziploc bags of dried fruit inside his snowsuit and walked, teetering, away from the gold he'd already uncovered. He dragged his shovel behind him through the snow.

He staggered into the frigid Antarctic wind for many miles, leaning into the wind and protecting his face with his arm. Even so, every whisker of his beard was, as it had been the day he'd started to dig, coated with ice—which made the beard very heavy and Bartholomew's neck very sore. He felt his body heat rising up and out of his body like smoke through a chimney. First he lost feeling in his toes. Then his shins. Then his knees.

He kept walking. One unfeeling foot after the other.

The sun rose and fell six times and he kept walking.

He walked until he'd eaten the last of the dried fruit (the very last piece being a stale and lumpy apple slice). Purple-toed, crimson-eared beneath his cap, and frostbitten in more places than he knew, he was ready—even desperate—to set up his tent and build a warm fire and be done with it all. He was just about satisfied he'd found all the treasure in Antarctica when the blade of his shovel scraped against something harder than ice.

He lifted the shovel high and drove it down into the snow. His shovel met something hard. Stopped. Made a ping noise. His unfeeling body vibrated like a plucked guitar string from the impact.

If his face hadn't been frozen stiff, Bartholomew would have smiled.

Again, he'd struck gold.

He kept digging.

* * *

Three years, two months, and sixteen days after first seeing something shiny poking through the South Pole snow, at 1:04 PM, Bartholomew sent word to the government of the United States of America that he may have found something big.

From the helicopter that lifted him back to the States, the soon-to-be-renowned American explorer looked down at his discovery. For the first time in one thousand, one hundred and seventy-two days—that's twenty-eight thousand, one hundred and twenty-eight hours or one million, six hundred and eighty-seven thousand, six hundred and eight minutes or one hundred and one million, two hundred and sixty thousand, and eight hundred frozen seconds—Bartholomew Rogers had time to think.

"What do we have here?" he mused aloud.

Of course what Bartholomew had found was not just gold. No, his discovery was much, much more important than just gold.

It was—you guessed it—a golden screw.

Chapter 7

This Very Year
(Twelve Years After Unscrewing Bart's Screw)

Whatta ya doin' outta bed, Calvin Cobble?"

Cal heard Berneatha Twiggins' voice even before he'd shinnied all the way up the fire pole to the ninth floor. He was in a hurry to make it back to his bed before the wake-up bell woke up his roommates and they saw he was gone.

There was no mistaking Berneatha's voice.

Berneatha was from Boston, Massachusetts, and she often pronounced the R sound softly, as if it were an H or a Y instead. She was sitting now, her back against the hallway wall, and looking right at Cal as he pulled himself up to the ninth floor. Berneatha's hair was, as always, pulled tight into long, braided pigtails. The gray T-shirt she wore was old and faded, and her jeans had holes in the knees.

No Hidden Shores orphan has a closet or dresser full of clothing options. In fact, Hidden Shores orphans wear the same clothes every day. The very clothes they wore the day a helicopter flew them through the hole in northeastern Alaska and dropped them off on the Pit of the Planet. They aren't clean clothes, either. There's only one washer and one drier at Hidden Shores, and both belong to the faculty. But Principal Warden certainly doesn't want to spend any of the orphanage's money on new clothes. (Or textbooks, for that matter. Each teacher writes his or her own textbook.)

Honestly, the orphans don't mind the smell; they've become accustomed to one another's body odor. And orphans learn to wash themselves with paper towels and hand soap when they use the bathroom once a day. The only problem with Principal Warden's system, then, is that young people have a persistent habit of growing; the clothes they wear when they're five or six are almost always too small by the time they're thirteen. This, however, isn't as much of a problem as you might think. When people are very young, they typically wear much baggier clothing than they do when they get older. And then there's the stretching. It just so happens that when you wear the same clothes every day—to class, to meals, and to bed—those clothes stretch to fit your similarly stretching bones. By the time orphans grow into teenagers, their shirts are a little thin and faded, but they do the job. Their pants are eventually too short, of course—nothing can be done about that—but, with the help of a pair of scissors, they transition easily into shorts. And shorts are more appropriate for the temperate Robert climate, anyway.

There are also exceptions. A few students do get "new" clothes. In every classroom in every school, there are those students who become adult-sized well before their classmates. By age twelve, there is inevitably a gawky six-foot girl who sits in the back so as not to block anyone's view of the chalkboard. These girls always make me think of plants, which grow toward the sun; if students were plants, I think to myself, the six-foot twelve-year-old girl's height would be easily explained: they'd be the ones who got the most sun. But students are not plants, and such things as height cannot be explained so conveniently. Nor can the fact that in every fifth- and sixth-grade classroom, there are always a couple boys who already have the mature, heavily muscled bodies of men. You know the ones: they've got those wide shoulders and thick necks. One of the great cruelties of childhood is that these large boys are so often the bullies. The ones who, generation after generation, steal smaller students' lunch money and candy and who threaten classmates into doing their homework for them. This is not always true—you may have a very amiable, gentle giant in your fifth- or sixth-grade class—but it is far too often the case that the giants are bullies. At Hidden Shores, the biggest boys were seventh-grader Hector Nelson, who had failed kindergarten three times outside the planet before arriving at Hidden Shores, and his eighth-grade friends. Hector and his friends intimidated with their size.

The point is that Hector, his friends, and a few tall girls at Hidden Shores grew out of their clothes and wore teachers' hand-me-downs—the antiquated and faded clothes teachers would otherwise throw away.

Berneatha was young and small enough that her pants were still full length; they were still pants—not capris or shorts. She wasn't wearing shoes, and her disproportionately large feet (when she did wear shoes, she wore men's seven and a half) looked even larger than usual in just her green socks, which weren't pulled on all the way and drooped off and under her toes.

Cal pulled himself up the fire pole a couple more feet and then jumped off to join his short, spirited friend on the ninth floor.

"I said, whatta ya doin' outta bed?"

"Ah—nothing, Bernie. What're you doing up here?" Though she was his best friend and a member of his seventh-grade class, Berneatha was only seven years old, and before the wake-up bell, she was supposed to be in the fourth-floor bedroom she shared with fourteen second-graders.

"I came up to say hello, but you weren't there." (With her heavy New England accent, Berneatha said it more like this: "I came up to say hello, but you went they.")

"You're not supposed to be out of bed, Bernie," Cal said. He tried to sound like Berneatha's babysitter as he said this, looking to flee the subject of where he'd been.

Berneatha stood up. She placed her hands at her sides, elbows jutting out. "And neither, Calvin Cobble, are you supposed to be outta bed," she said. "Where you been?" (It sounded like, "Way you been?")

"Nowhere," Cal said. Then he thought of a better answer: "I mean, I went to the bathroom, okay?"

There was only one one-person bathroom at Hidden Shores Orphanage—besides those in every teacher's room, which were off-limits to orphans—and it was on the first floor. Every Hidden Shores orphan had spent too many excruciatingly long minutes—rocking from foot to foot and trying to imagine hot, dry places like the Texas desert—waiting in a long line to use the bathroom. Taking all of this into consideration, it was not a terribly bad excuse Cal had come up with as his reason for being out of bed. Brainiac Berneatha could certainly see the logic in getting to the bathroom before everyone woke up and the mad dash to the toilet began, even if it meant risking getting caught and severely punished for being out of bed before the wake-up bell.

"Why didn't you just say so?" she said.

"Because," Cal said, "it's none of your business, Bernie." He knew if he told her where he'd been, she'd want to tag along and watch Mr. E skip stones. And that would ruin it for Cal. He loved that he was the only person in Bob, likely in the universe, who knew that crazy Mr. E could skip a stone all the way to the Mantle.

"I don't think I believe you, Calvin Cobble," Berneatha said. "Nah, that's not it. I think you're hiding something."

"Come on. I wouldn't hide anything from you," Cal said. "Honest." His forehead and cheeks were warm, and his feet were starting to sweat. The wake-up bell would sound soon, and they'd both be found out of bed and sent to Principal Warden's office. Not that Berneatha would care—she who had two years earlier met Cal during recess her first day at Hidden Shores and decided right then, on her own and with no adult's permission, that she would join his fifth-grade class. She had more nerve than Mighty Mouse, and the possibility of getting in trouble rarely deterred her. And Miss Trudy, their teacher, hadn't noticed there was a new student in the room, anyway. (Of course, even Berneatha would never do anything egregious enough that it might get her sent to the Shadow.)

"You know, Calvin Cobble, you don't have to tell me," said Berneatha, "but you certainly don't have to lie to me, either. You're insulting my intelligence."

And with that she stood up and skated in her green socks across the wood floor to the fire pole Cal had dismounted minutes before. It was, of course, an "up" pole, but Berneatha Twiggins never did care much for rules, and nobody was up and using the poles anyway. She jumped and slid down to the fourth floor. Her pigtails were the last parts of her to drop through the ninth-floor fire pole hole and out of sight. As Cal took his first step back toward his bedroom, he heard a voice muttering from below, in a thick Boston accent, "How rude . . . the bathroom? . . . if he thought I'd believe that garbage . . ."

Cal eased his bedroom door open and slipped into the room—a dim, rectangular space he shared with fourteen other seventh-grade boys. He tiptoed back to his bed, the fourth on the left, and was just pulling the covers over his shoes when he heard the wake-up bell's first toll of the morning.

* * *

Waiting his turn to slide down a fire pole for the second time that morning, Cal thought about Mr. E. He closed his eyes and saw the whole thing:

Mr. E's elaborate preparation.

The way his body coiled but his left arm stayed loose and ropey.

His purple tie swinging behind him in the opposite direction as his arm.

How he seemed to get every possible ounce of strength and power from his legs before he released his stone.

And, finally, Cal saw the stone bounce, bounce, bounce, bounce across the vast, flat lake, only stopping when it hit the black wall on the other side.

Chapter 8

Cal let go of the fire pole and joined the cafeteria breakfast line. He saw Berneatha up ahead of him. She'd already been served and was walking with her tray near one of the long walls of the rectangular cafeteria. Cal watched her march to the far corner of the room, pivot to her right, and continue marching. There were no tables or chairs between Cal and his friend.

One of Principal Warden's most prized programs at Hidden Shores Orphanage was "Meals on Legs." The idea was that if you ate while you walked instead of while you sat, you burned more calories.

"It's a healthier meal if you're eating and walking," the principal was fond of saying at all-school assemblies. Then he'd turn to the teachers and say, loud enough for students to hear, "And if the little mischief-makers are already moving, they're less likely to get antsy and start making mischief. And of course we save money not paying for tables and chairs."

So at every meal, after they got their food, Hidden Shores orphans organized themselves into a single-file rectangular line and walked around the cafeteria as they ate.

"Thank you, ma'am," Cal said to Mrs. Grossetta, the cafeteria cook who plopped Cal's breakfast onto his plate. Cal looked down at his tray and fought back the urge to vomit.

"Cheetah-cake" was the name the cooks at Hidden Shores had given to their own brand of egg dish—a massive sort-of-yellow block spotted with raisins. They'd come up with the recipe a year, two months, and six days ago (every orphan new the exact date of the dish's arrival), and they'd served nothing but cheetah-cake for every meal since. It covered various food groups, they said, and they could buy ingredients in bulk to save the school money. There was fruit in it, and it was a good source of protein.

Principal Warden approved.

Cheetah-cake may not be the worst tasting food of all time. Perhaps olive-loaf or lutefisk or gefilte fish or some secret family recipe somewhere is more repulsive. But cheetah-cake definitely, irrefutably, undeniably, invariably, and inevitably has the most disgusting consistency of any food humans have yet concocted.

The top and bottom of the cheetah-cake served for breakfast at Hidden Shores Orphanage are always, and intentionally, burned. Because the cooks burn the top and bottom of cheetah-cake, it isn't yellow like most egg dishes; it is sort-of-yellow—as orange and black as it is yellow.

In order to make it through the top and bottom layers of cheetah-cake, you maneuver the cake between the molars in the back of your mouth and bite down hard. The top and bottom are so thoroughly burned that you may wonder for an instant if you're biting through eggs or two sheets of plywood.

Once you gnaw through the top and bottom layers, you won't have to chew anything else that's burned. That probably sounds like good news.

It sounds like good news, but it isn't.

It is, in fact, very bad news.

The rest of the egg in cheetah-cake isn't burned, but it's not really cooked, either. The middle of cheetah-cake is hardly more than liquid eggs, no thicker or chewier than pancake batter.

And then you get to the raisins—as chewy and stale as old gum.

Cheetah-cake is all at once, then, about as hard as two sheets of plywood, as runny as pancake batter, and as rubbery as a piece of gum you find underneath your school desk or on the back of the bus seat in front of you.

When they first concocted cheetah-cake, the Hidden Shores cooks, Mr. and Mrs. Grossetta, proudly announced that they'd come up with yet another finger food (to go along with such delicacies they used to serve as frozen goulash on a stick). Finger food, they claimed, was environmentally friendly. By eliminating silverware from the equation, they explained, they saved on dishwater and soap.

Cal brought his breakfast to his mouth and bit down hard. The runny eggs in the middle squirted into his mouth even before he'd gnawed all the way through the burned outside layers. He gagged for a moment on a raisin that had wiggled its way into his throat.

When he looked up, he saw Fanny, the tall thirteen-year-old girl in line ahead of him, glaring back at him over her shoulder. She was wearing Miss Ecklebreck's old navy blue suit.

"Watch it, Firebrains. If you throw up on me, I don't know what I'll do," she said. "But trust me—you don't want me to find out."

After choking down his cheetah-cake and avoiding eye contact with Fanny for the rest of the meal (despite Fanny's frequent glances back at him), Cal turned his tray in to the dish room. Then he exited the cafeteria and shinnied up a fire pole to the ninth floor. He walked to the end of the hall to Miss Trudy's classroom for the beginning of what was shaping up to be a long day.

Chapter 9

Twelve Years Ago

Word spread quickly. The media got hold of the story and soon television news anchors, current-events and Antarctic-beat newspaper reporters, and citizens all over the world were talking about Bartholomew Rogers, the bearded American explorer who'd made the most surprising discovery since dinosaur bones.

People in all the world's countries talked about the flat-head screw despite initial challenges. The gold screw was too big for any adjective: "large," "huge," "enormous," "massive," "humongous," "vast," or even "Brobdingnagian" didn't capture its size relative to the other members of the screw family. So it became, simply, "Bart's Screw."

Once a name had been agreed upon, America dispatched a team of talented explorers to the North Pole. If there was a screw on the bottom of Earth, there was probably one on top, too. Seventy-three bright and brave adventurers and scientists were flown in the Air Force's fastest jets to Point Barrow, Alaska. From there they were carried, along with two state-of-the-art Navy submarines, aboard an aircraft carrier to the very top of the planet Earth.

The very top of Earth is not a landmass like the bottom of Earth. Surely you've heard that Santa and his elves live at the North Pole, and this is true. They live in a house made of candy, sing with holiday joy all the year round, keep reindeer that fly, and have and do all the marvelous, magical things you've likely learned they have and do. But Santa's North Pole is actually located at the northernmost tip of Greenland. Greenland is near the top of the world, and, contrary to its name, it is cold and snowy there every day of the year. If you no longer believe in jolly old Saint Nick and Rudolph the Red-Nosed Reindeer and their North Pole home, I suggest you take a trip to Greenland and see it all for yourself. It's not as hard to find as you might suspect, if you know what you're looking for.

Regardless, the geographic top of the world, the one important to this story, is not in Greenland. It's in the middle of the Arctic Ocean; in the middle, that is, of miles upon miles of frigid water. The water is so cold and deep it's almost black, and ice chunks float on top of it. It all looks, come to think of it, kind of like a great big glass of cola. And it was to the middle of this ocean that the seventy-three American adventurers and scientists were sent in Navy submarines to find the second screw.

After they got there, it took a whole day in the submarines to reach the ocean floor. It took another week to sweep off the sand and the octopus, squid, and cuttle-fish skeletons at the ocean's floor with strong mechanical brooms attached to the bottoms of the submarines especially for this important mission. After all that sand and all those skeletons had been swept aside, and smaller, more delicate and meticulous brushes had whisked away the remaining debris, the explorers found their gleaming golden screw, a precise duplicate of Bart's. They nicknamed this one "Santa's Screw."

Chapter 10

This Very Year
(Twelve Years After Unscrewing Bart's Screw)

"I see you have yet again, in blatant display of disrespect for me and your classmates, decided against combing your hair," Miss Trudy said to seventh-grade Cal as he entered her classroom. "Do you feel in some way empowered or invigorated by your rebelliousness, young man?"

Cal said the four words he'd repeated to his classroom teacher for six years: "I'm sorry, Miss Trudy," knowing that if he stood up for himself and tried to explain his situation, it would only make things worse. There was nothing he could do.

It was out of his control.

"Your actions, young man, belie your feigned apology. Do I not ask you every day to comb your hair? Yes. Yes, I do. And when you come to my class the next morning, is your hair not, once more, uncombed? Yes. Yes, it is. I reject your apology. Sorry simply is not good enough." She raised her chin and turned away from him. She patted her hair and tugged on her red flower-print dress. She muttered, "No doubt he gets this disrespectful nature from that father of his."

There it is again, Cal thought. Another mention of his father. What had he done that was so terrible? And why did every adult he encountered know more about his dad than he did?

His eyes on the classroom floor, Cal walked by Miss Trudy to his desk at the far side of the classroom. He smiled quickly at Berneatha, his friend, when he passed her desk in the middle of the room. She crossed her arms and looked away.

He sat down at his desk, next to the window, and removed *Trudy's Terrific Tasks*, the textbook Cal and his classmates had been working from since kindergarten.

"Fire!" yelled Hector Nelson, sitting behind Cal. Then Hector poured a plastic cup of lime Kool-Aid from the cafeteria on Cal's head.

The green Kool-Aid oozed off Cal's hair onto his face, neck, and shoulders.

Hector laughed. "Sorry, Torch, didn't know it was you. Thought your desk had caught on fire. Didn't want the building to burn down."

Other students laughed, too.

"His hair didn't even move," said Cicely, staring at Cal from the front of the room.

"Yeah—it's like the same as before, only now it's dripping green stuff," giggled Joe, sitting next to Cicely.

"It looks like alien blood," chimed Corretta, three desks over.

"I can't see," Mason complained from where he sat on the floor and against the wall near the pencil sharpener on the other side of the room. He hadn't had a desk since he went to the bathroom and Berneatha took his two years before. Really, he didn't mind; he always brought his pillow and sat on that. This way, low as he was and under Miss Trudy's line of sight, he was never called on to answer one of Miss Trudy's unanswerable questions. He slept through most lectures.

Cal feigned a smile and pretended to laugh, trying to play it cool. He was used to his classmates staring at him. He couldn't help squirming in his desk, though. Everything already felt sticky. His skin stuck to his T-shirt; his T-shirt stuck to his chair.

"You two young hellions stop that this instant," Miss Trudy said, tugging violently on her dress and glaring down at Cal and Hector over her horn-rimmed glasses. "I will not permit such behavior in my class. One more disruption, and I will send you both to see Principal Warden. If he wants both of you to spend the night on left side of the island, well, that will be his decision."

Cal gulped. He saw Belinda Poof stepping into the Shadow, never to be seen again. Did she just get lost in the dark? Did one of those murderous prisoners get her?

"Pops is over there," Hector said. "He wouldn't let nothing happen to me." Hector had never provided any proof that his father was a resident of Robert Inner-planet

Penitentiary (R.I.P.), but, knowing Hector, nobody doubted him. If anybody's dad was at the most maximum security prison in (or on) the world, it would be Hector's.

"Now. Where were we in our lesson?" Miss Trudy asked the class, patting her hair.

"We haven't even started yet," Berneatha said.

Miss Trudy looked at Berneatha, her eyes wide and incredulous. "No, no, young lady, you are mistaken. That cannot be right. Is it not at least lunchtime? I am quite sure I have already been in this classroom for several hours. Each of you has annoyed me a great deal today."

"Look at the clock, Miss Trudy," Brandon said, pointing to the wall.

"Young man, you will not tell me what to do—and you will raise your hand and wait for me to call on you," Miss Trudy said, glaring down at Brandon.

She looked at the clock.

"The clock says it is 8:34," Miss Trudy announced. "And if it is 8:34, then we must just be beginning our lesson now. Unless, of course, it is 8:34 in the PM?" Miss Trudy eyed her students suspiciously.

"Or I suppose one of you might have tampered with the clock so you would be permitted to listen to another of my famously entertaining lectures?"

She patted her hair proudly and tugged on her red flower-print dress.

"I suppose I will indulge you, then," she said. "Let us return to our lesson. Now. Where were we?"

Berneatha groaned.

Brandon raised his hand.

Mason lay back and closed his eyes.

Hector shoved the back of Cal's head.

Cal felt a sugary drop of Kool-Aid plop into his left ear and slide into his eardrum.

It was 8:34—well, now 8:35—in the morning. Cal had twelve hours and twenty-five minutes to go before lights out. Twelve hours and twenty-five minutes before he could close his eyes and know that when he opened them it would be morning and he'd get to watch Mr. E skip stones across Lake Arctic.

Chapter 11

At recess, standing in a group a healthy distance from Mr. Bruno, who was sitting and rolling a smoke as always on the front steps of the orphanage, Hector dared Bricks Boutwell to knock on Mr. E's door.

"Go see if the loon's home," he said. "Take his lawn mower for a spin while you're at it."

Bricks said he was tired; he'd do it tomorrow.

Of course he wasn't going to do it tomorrow, or the next day, or any other day. No Hidden Shores orphan would knock on Mr. E's door. Not even Hector. He was just talking tough.

Because while there was no place as scary to a Hidden Shores orphan as the Shadow, Mr. E's shack was the closest.

Chapter 12

Cal spent the afternoon looking out the classroom window and watching Mr. E mow the lawn. The sun shone off his bald head. He drove the lawn mower parallel to the shore, first toward the Shadow and then away. And then back again, the same thing, five feet closer to the orphanage this time. *How can he do that every day*, Cal thought. *Doesn't he get bored?*

And yet, Cal wished he was out there, mowing the lawn, doing the same thing over and over and over, instead of where he was, inside the orphanage, inside Miss Trudy's classroom.

Chapter 13

Twelve Years Ago

There was a mammoth golden screw on each end of Earth's axis, and nobody seemed to agree what should be done with either of them. Leaders of many countries expressed their opinions. Ultimately, it was the United States of America's decision, since American explorers made the odd discoveries.

When asked by a reporter what he thought should be done with the screws, Bartholomew Rogers snapped, "I don't care. Just leave me out of it. How did you get my phone number? You people, you just keep at it, don't you? Can't an explorer live his life in solitude these days?"

In congressional meetings, debate was heated.

"We should break 'em into pieces and use 'em to pay off our debts to other countries. They're made of gold, after all, aren't they?" said Representative Bull Bradford, a portly, bald-headed man from Alabama.

"We can always pay off debts. I say we use the screws'

grooves as landfills. We could take care of our garbage problem in a week," countered Representative Arnold Armstrong, a thin and mustached rancher from Montana.

The session escalated into a shouting match between many of the representatives, who all believed they knew the best course of action.

Now, up to this point, Representative Dorothy Dill had not said a word. She had been a federal legislator for only one year and, at thirty-eight, was the youngest representative in the room. Because of her relatively young age and limited congressional experience, and also because of her shy, thoughtful nature, Dorothy was often afraid to speak up. Of course it is the shy, thoughtful people who often have the most to say.

Dorothy finally mustered the gumption to raise her hand.

"Quiet. Quiet everyone," bellowed the Speaker of the House, who oversaw the meetings. "Representative Dill, what say you?"

Her voice no louder than a cat's purr, Dorothy said, "Why don't we unscrew them?"

The representatives, red-faced from arguing, considered the idea. Many sat down. For the first time all day, there was silence. Members of the United States House of Representatives saw logic in Dorothy's suggestion. Finally, Representative Evan Keel, a reasonable man who represented New Hampshire, ended the silence. "Representative Dill makes a lot of sense. Let's see what's underneath those screws."

"Yes—let's unscrew them!"

"I agree!"

"I concur!"

"It's the best idea I've heard yet!"

"It's what I was just about to say myself!"

The House had made its decision. In a week's time, they authored a bill and voted unanimously to unscrew Bart's Screw. They figured they'd unscrew the easy one first, then worry about the one at the bottom of an ocean. (Later, when the United States' elected officials figured out how they wanted to use Earth's core, Congress would authorize the building of the giant submarine screw *Arcticus*. The bloated, massively expensive Naval ship would be commissioned for one three-hour mission and then retired forever and always. It dropped down to Santa's Screw, unscrewed it six inches, and drained half the Arctic Ocean into the inside of Planet Earth. Then it tightened the screw back down and rose to the surface, never to be heard from again.) The House's excitement was contagious, and their bill also passed through the Senate unanimously. Citizens of America—and of most every other nation, as well—eagerly supported Congress's bill.

"What else is a screw for but to be unscrewed?" asked Lucy Lu, California homeowner and mother of four. Her question ran as the front-page headline for more than fifty thousand newspapers worldwide. Her words were translated in French, Spanish, Japanese, Swahili, and twenty-seven other languages. Just about every person on the planet agreed with Lucy: The world had to know what was underneath those screws.

By the time the President had the bill in his hands, he had almost no choice but to sign it. He sat proudly behind his desk in the Oval Office, eager to please his curious citizens.

Television cameras zoomed in on the President's hand and pen as he scribbled his name above the dotted line at the bottom of the bill.

Continents trembled and oceans and lakes rippled as billions of people cheered.

Chapter 14

"Can you feel that?" Ron Cobble asked his wife, Julia. "It feels like we're standing on a—a—well, something that shakes." He always had trouble finding the right word.

"Like the tip of a tuning fork, maybe?" Julia helped him out. They smiled; she always knew what he meant. "Or a dance floor? Perhaps it feels like a minor earthquake?"

"One of those, yeah."

It was a summer evening, cool but not cold. The falling sun was turning the sky all sorts of colors: bubble gum pink, tangerine peel orange, grape jelly purple. They were walking home from Cone On In!, the little ice cream shop they'd frequented that month. Julia was pregnant, and she constantly craved ice cream. This evening, she licked all the way around a scoop of chocolate chip. Ron took his time with his cone of black cherry.

"Did you hear the President signed that bill today?" Julia asked her husband. The Cobbles were hardly aware of the screws that had captured the rest of the world's attention. They were young and in love, just two years into their marriage and two months away from the birth of their first child. They were too happy and busy with their own lives to be concerned with the goings-on at the bottom of the planet. They didn't know that evening that it would be their last walk together. They didn't know that Julia would never again see her husband without handcuffs jangling on his wrists. That, suddenly bedridden in a hospital due to complicated final stages of her pregnancy, she would watch her husband fail to give the right and true answer to the judge's important question. They knew none of this as they walked home from Cone On In!

No, this night they walked hand in hand, eating ice cream, and everything was right in their world.

"That's right," Ron answered. "They're going to pull out Ben's Nail."

"You mean Bart's Screw," Julia corrected. "They're going to unscrew Bart's Screw."

"Right, yeah—Bart's Screw. Of course."

They walked and enjoyed the summer and each other's company.

"Hey," Ron said, "did you read about Angry Armadillo in this afternoon's paper?"

"I read about Mad Mutt. He killed another security guard—and they still haven't caught him."

"What a relief!" Ron exclaimed.

Julia gave him her corrective stare.

"I mean a shame," Ron said.

Both looked to the sky. The hues of pink and orange and purple were getting darker.

"Beautiful moonrise tonight, don't you think?" Ron asked.

Julia smiled. She decided to let her husband's mistake go. It was actually a lovely way of looking at it, she thought.

Months later, watching her husband stand trial for a series of ghastly crimes, Julia would take some comfort in the word. Then, as on the evening of their walk to and from the town ice cream parlor, Julia would close her eyes and say the word softly, recording it in her memory: "Moonrise."

Chapter 15

This Very Year
(Twelve Years After Unscrewing Bart's Screw)

Cal never did sleep much. Most nights he lay on his bed, listening to his roommates inhale and exhale as he gazed out the ninth-floor bedroom window at the few stars aligned with the hole in northeastern Alaska that night.

He didn't know what kept him awake. His thoughts rolled over and dropped off his brain like rivers rushing to a waterfall, never staying put long enough for Cal to identify them before they were carried away from him, and he finally fell, as if in a barrel on one of those rivers, into fitful sleep. Perhaps it was loneliness that kept him awake much of the night, the searing, enduring sense that he didn't, and never would, fit in. Perhaps it was guilt. Though he had never met his parents, he knew his mother had died during labor as she brought him to the world. So she would still be alive if it weren't for him. Sometimes, when he closed his eyes, he saw Belinda Poof. When he saw her, it was always the same image: her last stride into the Shadow—half of her leg gone and then all of her. Why didn't he yell out to her? Why didn't he do anything? And then again, on some of those nights, different unanswered questions kept him awake. Why was he down here? Where was his father? Why hadn't his father ever come for him? Why had he abandoned his wife and soon-to-be-born son?

One of those nights, not that long ago, as Cal stared from his bed out the window at the waxing half-moon, something had tapped him on the shoulder and then nudged him out of bed. That something drew him to the bedroom window, through which he saw Mr. E skip a stone for the very first time. And finally, unexpectedly, that something had bidden Cal to come closer, had convinced him he needed a better view.

A talented educator might call that something Curiosity. The talented educator would use all the tools at her disposal to dig a path for Curiosity, to encourage it to visit her classroom each day. The talented educator knows that Curiosity is a gift—one that can never truly be killed. She knows that if she looks closely, she'll find it. It won't take her long to figure out who the curious ones are in her class. It's the way they look at things, she'll tell you. She'll say that Curiosity lives in the observers among us, the children and adults who watch and learn and see things from unique perspectives.

A true observer, after all, is always curious. As the observer observes, he asks: How does he do that? How and why does that happen? And, inevitably, Can I do that? Cal, against all odds, was an observer. He asked himself these very questions as he watched Mr. E pace Robert's beach, so thoroughly engaged in his remarkable hobby of skipping stones across the biggest lake in the world.

The talented educator understands that when Curiosity visits a classroom, magic materializes, sparks spit, learning lights up the space. The talented educator admires and encourages Curiosity. The more intimate the student's relationship with Curiosity, wisdom tells her, the deeper the student's engagement with the subject matter. The talented educator dreams of a classroom full of observers, of young people who ask "How?" and "Can I do that?"

Miss Trudy, the round and lumpy teacher who had followed Cal and his classmates from their first year at Hidden Shores all the way to the seventh grade, was not a talented educator. Miss Trudy most certainly did not value Curiosity.

Miss Trudy believed that regarding a child, Curiosity was inappropriate, threatening, and, above all, annoying. In truth, she cared more about her bouffant hairstyle than she did about her students. I'm sure you've seen women with bouffant hairstyles before. The bouffant is a carefully puffed-out style worn by many elderly women with thinning hair. In the end, their hair looks like a kernel of popped popcorn. Miss Trudy was always patting her popcorn-kernel hair with her pudgy, short-fingered hands, making sure it looked just right. She was also always tugging on her flower-print dress, straightening it where it bunched at her waist. She had seven differently colored flower-print dresses, one for each day of the week. Teachers and students at Hidden Shores didn't get weekends off, after all. And she always called her students "young man" or "young lady" because she never took the time to learn their names.

"If you would all shut your mouths and listen to me, you would not be so stupid," she'd said at least twelve times a day, every day, since Cal's class first met her. "I am trying to help you, but you just will not listen, will you?" She patted her hair and tugged on her flower-print dress as she said this.

The truth is that Miss Trudy was scatterbrained, and her lessons could be hard to follow.

Cal had gotten on Miss Trudy's bad side right from the start, as a kindergartner.

The class had been learning the lowercase alphabet that day six years ago. Miss Trudy had written, in neat printing, all the letters from a to z on the blackboard. When they got to the letter w, five-year-old Cal had gotten confused. Why, he wondered, was it called a double-u when it looked like a double-v? He raised his hand to ask.

"What?" Miss Trudy said, looking down at Cal over her horn-rimmed glasses, dropping her piece of chalk on the blackboard tray. "What in the world is it, young man?"

"I—I have a question," Cal said.

"What do you mean, you have a question?"

"A-about the double-u, Miss Trudy. Why—"

"I do not allow questions in my classroom," interrupted Miss Trudy. "About the alphabet or anything else. It is my experience that the student asking the question never knows as much as the teacher answering it. Why should I spend my time listening to you go on regarding a subject about which I am already knowledgeable and you are not?"

Cal's face became hot and red. "Oh. I—I'm sorry," he said.

"Sorry? I do not care if you are sorry, young man. Sorry won't give me back my time." She turned back to the blackboard. She muttered, "No, I absolutely do not allow questions in my classroom," as she patted her hair and tugged on her blue flower-print dress.

But instead of picking up her piece of chalk and moving on to the next letter, x, she turned back around, narrowed her eyes, and looked down at Cal once more. "And do you know what else I do not allow in my class? Students with uncombed hair. Why have you not combed your hair like your classmates? Do you see yourself as superior to them—or, heaven forbid, superior to me?"

"I—I did comb my hair, Miss Trudy, it just—it just won't stay."

"And now you are lying to me. The nerve! You clearly have not combed your hair, and yet you say you have. You are a liar, young man. A questioner and a liar. And worst of all, you are slovenly and lazy and have no self-respect, as you neglect to comb your own hair. Leave this classroom and do not come back until your hair has been combed."

Miss Trudy had grown irritated with Cal every day for the next six years. Because every day he came to class with his hair messier than it had been the day before.

Chapter 16

Cal pushed back his sheet and blanket and slid surreptitiously out of bed. He was already dressed. He'd gotten into the habit of wearing his capris, socks, and shoes to bed. Not having to change in the morning made sneaking out quicker and safer.

He tiptoed across the room.

He carefully—oh, so carefully—opened the door, just a crack.

He turned and looked around the room to make sure his roommates weren't watching.

He backed out of the room.

He closed the door softly, with his fingertips.

He turned. Right into Berneatha Twiggins.

"Going to the bathroom again, Calvin Cobble?" Berneatha said, her right eyebrow raised so it looked like an upside-down smile.

"Uh—yeah," Cal said, his heart trying to recover

from the jolt it had been dealt by Berneatha's surprise appearance. "Shouldn't have had that glass of water before I went to bed."

"You'd think you would have learned that yesterday."

"Yeah. I guess I forgot, Bernie."

Shoeless Berneatha grinned. "Well, I have to go, too."

"You have to go where?" Cal said.

"To the bathroom. I'm going down there with you." (She said it, "I'm goin' down they with you.") Berneatha looked pleased with herself.

"I think I can manage by myself, thanks."

When Berneatha cocked her head and raised her eyebrow, Cal understood that he wasn't going to see Mr. E skip stones that morning. There was nothing he could do about it. But he wanted to see Mr. E skip stones tomorrow morning, so all he said was, "Okay, Bernie, sure. Just be quiet about it."

He tiptoed as carefully as ever to the third fire pole. Berneatha skated in her too-big socks behind him. When he slid down the pole, she was right behind—or, actually, above—him still. When he dropped to the cafeteria floor, he moved out of the way so Berneatha had room to touch down.

Mr. and Mrs. Grossetta made their usual morning noise in the kitchen, opening and closing ovens and chanting hoarsely along to another folk song playing low on the radio.

Steam poured through the cracks above and below the kitchen door and settled briefly near the cafeteria ceiling before the nearest fire pole holes sucked the steam up and out of sight.

The air smelled salty and tangy.

"Not again," Berneatha said. "If I need to eat cheetah-cake for one more meal, I'm going on a hunger strike."

"Like nobody's tried that?" Cal asked. "How well has it worked for anyone else?"

Berneatha put her hands on her hips and opened her mouth to respond when Cal put a finger to his lips, the universal sign for "Shh. Be quiet," and pointed across the empty rectangular room to the bathroom on their right, next to Principal Warden's office (which was connected to his bedroom and surely his own private bathroom). "You go first," he whispered.

Berneatha didn't move.

"Come on," Cal whispered, "go." He swiveled his head as an owl does, surveying his surroundings, looking for predators (such as tone-deaf cooks and a volcanic-tempered principal).

"I don't need to."

"What do you mean, you don't need to?"

"Just what I said, Calvin Cobble." Berneatha's voice rose. "I don't need to use the bathroom."

"Then why'd you come down here with me?"

"'Because I didn't believe you were coming down here to use the bathroom, that's why." Her voice was a whisper-shout now, about as loud as her regular speaking voice only hoarser.

"You've got to be kidding me," Cal said under his breath.

Just then he sensed danger. He'd never felt so far from safety as he did now, having a hushed conversation in the middle of an almost silent, empty room, with adult cooks in the kitchen to Cal's left, and Principal Warden in his office to Cal's right.

To get out of the middle of the room, Cal said, "Well, I'm going." He walked briskly over the tile floor to the bathroom door, opened it, and went in. (The bathroom, like every other room at Hidden Shores, including Principal Warden's office, remained unlocked at all times. As a matter of fact, Hidden Shores Orphanage didn't have locks. The principal believed that when students had enough respect for authority, you didn't need locks. Indeed, no orphan ever broke into his office. Not that there was anything in there worth stealing, anyway— nothing worth the risk of finding out what would happen if Principal Warden caught you where you weren't supposed to be.) Once inside the bathroom, Cal wasn't sure if he should just wash his hands for a long time or what. He didn't have to go to the bathroom, and he didn't want to make a lot of noise. Usually by this time of the morning he was off in his own world with Aunt Robbie, her safe and shaded arms wrapped around him, hiding and protecting him.

Cal hadn't been in the bathroom ten seconds when the door opened behind him and Berneatha came speed-skating in, shutting the door quickly but gently behind her. Cal hardly had the space or time to turn around and face her.

"What are you doing, Bernie?" Cal whispered. "I thought you didn't have to use the bathroom."

The bathroom was tiny, four feet long and four feet wide, with a toilet and a sink crammed in somehow. Cal's chin pressed into Berneatha's forehead as he waited for her answer.

"He's out there," she said into his chest. For the first time that morning, her voice was soft.

"What? Who's out there?" Cal whispered back.

"Principal Warden. I heard him opening his door, and I ran in here."

"Oh, great. Now what're we gonna do?" Cal knew if they were caught, he'd probably never see Mr. E skip stones again. "He's not coming in here, is he?"

"Beats me," Berneatha said. "If you wouldn't a been so loud out there, Calvin Cobble, maybe he wouldn't a come out at all."

"Me? If I wouldn't a been so loud?" Cal said. "Since when are you scared of Principal Warden, anyway?"

"I—I don't know. It just seems like we shouldn't be down here, you know? There's a big difference between getting caught up on your floor and getting caught on his, I guess. And I don't even know what we're doing. If I'm gonna get in trouble, I at least wanna know what for."

Cal stared helplessly over Berneatha's pig-tailed head at the door, waiting to be busted.

When nothing happened, Berneatha turned—wedging

one of her elbows between two of Cal's ribs in the process—and got down on her stomach. She peered into the cafeteria through the space between the bottom of the door and the bathroom's tile floor. The bathroom was small enough that she had to bend her legs so that her shins ran parallel with the wall opposite the door. The empty toes of her socks touched the wall.

Cal hopped onto the toilet and crouched on the cover.

"He walked into the kitchen," Berneatha said. "The door's swinging shut. Must be talking to the cooks."

Berneatha squinted her eyes to see better.

"Let's go," she said.

"Go? Are you serious?"

"I'm going," Berneatha said, rising to her knees and then feet. "I don't know about you, but I'm not gonna hang out in a dirty bathroom all morning. Something tells me someone'll find us, regardless—unless two-hundred sixty-eight orphans suddenly come down with constipation all at once." She opened the door and ran to the nearest fire pole.

Cal wasn't sure what to do, so he jumped off the toilet and followed her.

Out in the cafeteria again, with no place to hide, he heard Principal Warden's voice: "Well, whatever it is, Mr. and Mrs. Grossetta, it smells delicious to my wallet. Cheap, cheap, cheap. That's the goal, as you well know."

Cal waited nervously for Berneatha, who was small and therefore slow going up the poles, to shinny up far enough that he could grab hold of the pole and start shinnying. He kept his eyes on the kitchen door all the while. By the time he had his legs wrapped around the pole, he could see the shadow of Principal Warden's feet in the crack under the door.

Cal flew up the fire pole like it was a race and the prize was a trip away from the cereal box-shaped orphanage to the Earth's surface. He hopped off on the second floor. Three seconds later, he heard Mr. and Mrs. Grossetta singing, their voices louder through the swung-open door. Twelve seconds later, he watched Principal Warden walk under the fire pole hole back to his office.

"How slow are you, Bernie? I barely made it up here before he walked by."

"Well, why'd you use the same pole I did? Not like you didn't have other options."

Berneatha had a point. "Because this one was . . . closest," Cal whispered. "Anyway, it doesn't matter. I'm going back to my room."

"I thought you had to use the bathroom," Berneatha said.

"Yeah, well, Principal Warden scared the pee out of me."

Berneatha rolled her eyes but jumped up on the pole and shinnied up to the fourth floor to her bedroom and fourteen sleeping seven-year-old girls.

Cal went to the next "up" pole, watched Berneatha hop off when she got to her floor, and kept shinnying all the way up to the ninth floor.

As Cal tiptoed back to his bedroom door, he felt

strangely steeled—not shaken—by the morning's almost-encounter with the principal.

Instead of opening his bedroom door, he turned and walked back to the third fire pole.

He was going to see Mr. E skip his stones.

Chapter 17

By the time Cal made it out the front door, he knew he was several minutes late for the big event. He sprinted across the front lawn and scuttled up Aunt Robbie's spine. He didn't want to miss seeing Mr. E skip his first stone of the morning.

Sitting in his usual perch, Cal looked out through the maple leaves and tried to spot Mr. E pacing across the rock beach.

But Mr. E wasn't pacing. So used to seeing the tall man gliding back and forth along the shoreline of Lake Arctic, it took Cal a moment to locate him. Once Cal spotted him, he had to rub his eyes to make sure he was really seeing what he thought he was seeing.

Mr. E was standing still on the beach, looking in the direction of the orphanage—in the direction, more precisely, of Aunt Robbie the maple tree. *He's not looking at me, is he?* Cal wondered, a sudden panic seeping into his bones. His body suddenly as stiff as the maple tree branch upon which he sat.

"Hey, you," Mr. E said.

Oh, no, Cal thought. He reminded himself that he wasn't absolutely, positively, without-a-doubt sure that Mr. E had seen him. Maybe he was talking to a squirrel or something. Then Cal remembered there were no squirrels in Robert.

"Yeah, you," Mr. E said, "up in that tree. Why don't you come on down and introduce yourself? Then I'll do the same."

Oh, no, Cal thought again.

Busted, he clambered deliberately down to the ground. In order to get down out of Aunt Robbie, Cal usually slid down her trunk, but this morning he used every handhold and foothold he could find. What would Mr. E do to him? Would he bawl Cal out for spying on him and being up before the wake-up bell? Or, worse, would he report him to Principal Warden? Would he tie Cal to a tree in the Shadow, leaving him for the murderers and whatever else lived out there? Would Mr. E do something even worse than that? Cal didn't know exactly what even worse than that meant, but not knowing made it harder to stomach.

Cal was only certain about one thing: Everyone said Mr. E was crazy.

And if he was as crazy as everyone said he was, he was probably capable of doing anything.

Would he force Cal under water until he drowned

and then lock him up in his little shack and wait for his corpse to decompose? Would he skip Cal's bones across Lake Arctic to hide the evidence? Would he chew Cal up with his lawn mower and use his remains as fertilizer? *Not that anyone would look for me anyway,* Cal thought. He wished he had Bernie with him. She'd at least put up a fight. Here he was, marching across Hidden Shores' long front lawn to a certain death like he was magnetized to the rocks there and had no choice.

Like everything else, it was out of his control now.

He walked with his head down, not daring to look up. Too soon, he was looking down at dark bare feet. Cal noticed that the toenails were neatly clipped and that the outside edges of the big toes were callused. The calluses were grass stained.

"Well, why don't you look up here, son." He heard Mr. E's voice from above. "Awful hard holding a conversation without looking at one another."

Cal looked up from Mr. E's bare feet. First at his shins. Then up his black dress pants to his knees. Then his waist, where his gray-striped white dress shirt was tucked into the pants in some places and not in others. Then Cal looked up at Mr. E's stomach. Then his chest. His wide, wide shoulders. Up and up Cal looked. Mr. E was so tall Cal couldn't see the sun behind him. Just the water of Lake Arctic and the Mantle, dark and cracking orange, that framed it all. Finally, Cal looked up and into Mr. E's dark, hollow face. He was surprised to see Mr. E's lips curled into a smile.

"How 'bout I start, then?" Mr. E said. "You can call me Mr. Englewood. And, if I may ask, what moniker is it you go by?"

From somewhere deep inside his throat—hiding in his vocal folds, perhaps—Cal found his voice, but it didn't say what he wanted it to say.

"E for Englewood," Cal mumbled.

"Excuse me?" Mr. E's eyes narrowed, and his brow furrowed.

"I—I mean I'm Calvin Cobble, Mr. E—Mr. Englewood. I guess most people call me Cal."

Mr. Englewood's eyes flickered recognition. "Cobble, huh?" he said to himself. Then his focus returned to Cal.

"Glad to know you, Cal," he said, extending his hand. "How you doin'?"

"Ah—pretty good, I guess. I mean, good, sir, thanks," Cal answered. He shook Mr. Englewood's hand. The hand was hard and warm and dry.

"Good, huh? Thought you was in trouble or somethin', way you hotfooted it to that maple."

"You mean you saw me before I got to the tree?" He'd had it figured out in his head that Mr. Englewood had seen him through Roberta's leaves. That's when Cal had first seen Mr. Englewood, anyway.

"Been hard to miss you with that mane of yours." The tall man smiled now. "Guess you could say I didn't catch you red-handed, though. No, I caught you red-headed." He chuckled to himself.

Cal grinned, or at least smiled, too. Then there it was:

a laugh of his own. It was a small laugh, one that barely made it out of his mouth. But he wasn't faking the smile or the laugh like he had in Miss Trudy's classroom the day before. He really was smiling. And he really was laughing. It was the first time in a long while that Cal had been able to laugh about his hair. It was pretty hard to laugh about something that was always getting him in trouble. But something about the way Mr. Englewood said it, without accusing or ridiculing, put Cal at ease.

"I take it you're looking to give stone-skipping a try," Mr. Englewood said, flipping a stone with his thumb into the air as if it were a coin and grabbing it out of the air with the other hand. "Am I right?"

"Uh, yeah, okay, I mean, if you're sure, I don't want to interrupt—but I don't know how."

"Well, Mr. Cal Cobble, you got yourself some fine conditions for learning."

Mr. Englewood turned and walked toward the water, motioning that Cal should join him.

His purple tie wagged behind him.

Chapter 18

Y ou see that water out there? That's as quiet as you'll ever see water, unless it's in a glass." Mr. Englewood was standing near the water and facing his shack, as Cal had seen him do so many times before. "And that's the way it always is here on this great big bobber. It just so happens it's the perfect place to skip a stone. You don't wanna throw your stones into choppy water, see; those waves got minds of their own—can make your stone jump instead of leap. Sometimes a wave'll swallow your stone whole." Mr. Englewood looked pained thinking about it. "But you can't control the water. You cannot. You should consider yourself lucky to be where you're at."

Lucky to be where I'm at? Cal thought.

Mr. Englewood continued: "What you can control is the stone you throw. Sure, just about any stone you find'll skip, long as it's not too big and you can't get it going fast enough—or too small, because then you run in

to the same problem. But if you're looking to skip something more than once or twice, you need to find the right
stone. You're looking for something that's flat and not too
sharp."

"Okay," Cal said. "I think—I think I can do that."

But he wasn't sure Mr. Englewood heard him. His
teacher was getting into a rhythm now. His left arm
swung in front of him, as if being dragged by the stone he
held between his pointer finger and thumb.

"Makes sense, doesn't it? Flatter your stone is, easier
time it has skimming over the water. Like when you do a
big belly flop and your body doesn't sink right away. With
a flat stone, you just spreading out the surface area. The
more of it touches the water, the better. And you don't
want the corners to be too sharp, or your fingers'll start to
hurt, and you won't be out here long."

"Right," Cal said. This time he was sure Mr.
Englewood hadn't heard him. It was like he'd been
tape-recorded and Cal had hit the "play" button. Mr.
Englewood stopped at the appropriate times, but it didn't
really matter how Cal answered; he was going to get the
same lesson regardless. Cal wondered if Mr. Englewood
had wanted to tell someone all of this for a long time.

"And that's the whole point, now, isn't it? You want to
be out here for a while. Or if you can't stay out long, you
at least want to keep from getting a sore arm that prevents
you from skipping tomorrow. When you skip stones, you
get in touch with everything around you. Sure, it's challenging. But it's relaxing, too. Challenging and relaxing.

Bet you can't say that about too many things, huh? No, sir. There's nothing quite like it. Just you and your thoughts and a whole lot of water. The water shushing everyone, saying, 'Hey there—quiet. Now's not the time for talking.' That's why it's best to skip alone."

He paused. He looked down at Cal from his great height and grinned.

"I don't mean you got to be by yourself, Cal Cobble. I'm glad for the company. Really. All I mean is you got to get away from all the adults taking their photographs and kids squawking louder than the gulls. I got nothing against little kids, mind you. I even like their squawking. You've got some delightful squawkers up in your school. I hear them when you all have recess. It's just you don't skip stones until you're old enough to be silent for a time, that's all."

Cal nodded. He'd never seen any of the teachers at Hidden Shores use a camera, and there were no gulls to be found anywhere on the island of Robert. At least not on the lighted half, and he wasn't about to start planning a field trip to the Shadow to find out if there were gulls in there. But he knew what Mr. Englewood meant about silence. He'd been sneaking out of the orphanage for over two months so he could be alone and not have to talk to anybody.

"Once you find yourself a good-looking flat stone, then you walk up to the water. You dig your feet in so you're not tripping all over yourself."

Mr. Englewood dug his feet in. Cal mirrored him, digging his feet in, too.

"You bend your knees."

Mr. Englewood did this. As did Cal.

"Then you shift all your weight over to your back leg. That's where you gonna get all your power."

Cal watched Mr. Englewood lean against his back leg so that the heel of his front foot lifted up, only the toes still touching the rocks. Cal did the same.

"When you got all your power stored up in your back leg so it's like a coiled spring, you're ready. You push off and use all that power and throw the stone, submarine-style, arm as close to the ground as you can get it, transferring all your weight over to your front foot. You wanna throw it low so it stays close to the water, and you want to throw it out as far as you can, 'cuz once it hits that water, it'll start to slow in a hurry. You ever see one of them big airplanes land? Soon's it hits the runway, it opens up brake panels on its wings—called spoilers, if you wanna know—and slows itself down. Your stone's kinda like that. When it hits the water, it slams on its breaks and throws up its spoilers, in a manner of speaking."

Then he did it. He threw his stone as a demonstration. Cal pantomimed him, throwing an imaginary stone with his right hand and following through up high, by his ear.

Cal watched Mr. Englewood's stone cut through the air, pretending for a moment that it was his stone. That he'd sent it whizzing above the water like a bullet. Even when he reminded himself that it wasn't his stone, after all, he still couldn't quite believe that he was actually standing next to its thrower. As thrilling an experience as it always was to watch Mr. E from Roberta's safe branches, it didn't compare, Cal now realized, to watching the whole thing up close.

When the stone finally glided down to the water, right on top of the trail of morning sunlight, Cal heard the sound it made more clearly than ever before. "Hear that?" Mr. Englewood's gentle voice sounded distant as Cal concentrated on the stone bounding across Lake Arctic. "Sounds kinda like a drum beat, doesn't it?"

He was right. It was like someone across a big room had tapped a pillow with a drumstick. The tapper's beat sped up but softened until it was finally undetectable.

"But there's nobody out there marching in no fancy costume," said Mr. Englewood.

Cal saw Mr. Englewood get down on his stomach and tilt his head so his ear was right next to the water. He looked back at Cal, smiling big.

"Down here," he said. He motioned Cal over with his hand.

Cal took two steps toward Mr. Englewood.

"Down on your stomach, Cal. You wanna hear it, don't you?"

Cal joined his teacher, face down on the rock beach. He tilted his head so his left ear was close to the water.

He listened. What he heard surprised him. He heard bum-bum bum-bum bum-bum. Then he realized it was his heart he was hearing, not the skipping stone.

"Tell that metronome in your chest to slow its beat, Cal," Mr. Englewood said. "It's good you excited, but you're not gonna hear nothing if that thing keeps pop-pop-popping away."

Cal tried to relax. He concentrated on listening to Lake Arctic's waves as they nudged up against the shore and then retreated.

His heartbeats slowed, quieted.

Then there it was.

Ta . . . . . ta . . . . ta . . . ta . . . the beats close together but softer each time.

"That stone's up on its edge now. Soon it's gonna be one sound; you gonna hear it stop bouncing out there and start skiing."

Up on its edge, the stone's song was long and steady and still whispery, like when you exhale after a deep breath.

The stone was far, far out of sight now. The sound that made it back to Bob's shore was the softest sound Cal had ever heard, he was sure of it. He stretched his neck and strained to hear it better as it moved away from him. He'd never listened so carefully to anything in the world. He tilted his head and moved his ear even closer to the water. He was listening so hard his forehead hurt. Some of his wild red-orange hair, sticking out sideways like trampled tall grass, pierced the surface of the water.

THWACK!

The relatively loud sound of the stone hitting the Mantle—which, from where Cal and Mr. Engelewood lay, was actually about as loud as the sound this book makes when you snap it closed (after you've finished this chapter and inserted a bookmark so you remember where you left off)—startled Cal into flinching. When he flinched, his head dropped under water—hair, left ear, cheek, chin, eye, and nose.

SPLOOSH!

When he lifted his head, he heard laughter. He wiped his left eye dry with the heel of his hand and looked over at Mr. Englewood, still lying next to him.

"Stone got the best of you today, huh, Cal?" Mr. Englewood's eyes were bright, his smile wide. "You look like a wet porcupine, son. Your hair responds to water about like a bunch of prickly quills." He sat up, laughing so hard he had to brace himself with his hands so he didn't fall over backward. Still laughing, he got to his feet, extended his hand, and helped Cal to his feet.

"That's about as much excitement as I can take for one day. That okay with you, Cal? Based on the hurry you were in to get out here, I'd bet it's about time for you to be getting back, anyway. Am I right?"

Cal nodded.

Mr. Englewood's eyes were still laughing. "I assume you're coming back tomorrow? To try skipping a stone for yourself?"

Cal's heart leapt in his chest. "Okay," he said. "Yeah. Thanks, Mr. Englewood."

"You head back home, and I'll see you tomorrow. Oh. And don't bother hiding up in that maple tree. We don't got time for none of that nonsense. Just walk right on over here. I can turn my back if you really don't want to be seen." He laughed again, then he gave Cal a pat on the back and headed for his shack.

Walking toward the big front door of Hidden Shores Orphanage, Cal turned and watched Mr. Englewood glide back to his shack, framed as he walked by the Mantle's dark proscenium and spotlighted by the sunlight for an instant, as if on stage. Cal listened to Mr. Englewood laughing. *He was right*, Cal thought. *A stone did get the best of me*. And then a peculiar thing happened. For the second time that morning, Cal laughed, too.

Chapter 19

Twelve Years Ago

On the day Bart's Screw was set to be unscrewed, there were more human beings in Antarctica than there had been if you were to add up all the people who'd been there on every day since the sixteenth century, when humans first explored Earth's coldest continent. Antarctica's is a brutal history. Many have lost their lives at the South Pole. Others have survived on foul-tasting penguin meat. It was, then, a rather remarkable occasion when hundreds of thousands of people bought tickets to board big boats built especially for the perilous trip through iceberg-infested waters to the South Pole.

Bartholomew Rogers' new book, *How to Survive a Day at the Bottom of the World*, was an international bestseller, and many of the people at the South Pole had the book with them, stashed in a backpack or a zippered jacket pocket. (The book's popularity came despite the author's reclusive life. Bartholomew himself had never once appeared on television or given an interview to promote his book. He had remained out of the public's view, right when his celebrity could have made him rich. Whenever he was tracked down, he always muttered something unfit for publication.) People had taken to heart much the advice Bartholomew offered in *How to Survive*. After the title page of the lime-green edged book and before the first chapter, he'd included a bold-printed list of Three Important (and Simple!) Things to Remember for Antarctic Survival. Number one was

Wear lime-green. Lime-green repels cold air.

Just about every person in Antarctica was, as instructed, clad entirely in lime-green. It was a sight to behold—as many people as there are in the city of Minneapolis, dressed identically in bright lime-green, standing in a circle around a gleaming golden screw with a head the size of Rhode Island. A twenty-seven-foot chain-link fence with padlocked doors and barbwire festooned at the top separated the people from the flat golden head. National guards, each wearing a puffy lime-green jumpsuit, stood on either side of each entrance. Authorities didn't want anyone venturing too near the groove and falling to their death.

"When's he coming, Jeff?" asked an asthmatic twelve-year-old boy named Herschel, the youngest and smallest and likely most courageous of all the hundreds of thousands of very courageous people who'd gathered to see Bart's Screw unscrewed.

"The big man's supposed to be here real soon. Any minute now," answered his older brother, Jeffrey, looking at his watch. " 'Least, that's what they said on the news."

"He's already been down here, you know," said Herschel, who knew everything there was to know about Bart's Screw. He pumped his inhaler and breathed in its medicine, gathering strength to continue. "He came down with all them pro football players, remember? It was on the news. They shoveled out the groove as charity work or somethin."

"Strange charity work."

"Yeah. You're right." Herschel had never thought about it. It was strange charity work. "Hey, Jeff, how do you think they're gonna do it?"

"What?"

"You know"—he pumped his inhaler, sucked in the medicine—"unscrew it."

Really, no one in Antarctica that day knew how a screw of such size could be unscrewed. There was certainly no screwdriver big enough for the task. Some suggested digging around the screw until they reached its bottom tip. Others guessed the screw was too big, and it would take too long to dig around it—months or even years. Still others suggested blowing the screw up with dynamite. To most, this seemed more foolish. What a waste it would be to blow up the greatest gold discovery of all time! Plus, the whole point of unscrewing Bart's screw was to find out what was underneath it. If they blew the screw up, how could they be sure they wouldn't blow up whatever it was they were trying to find?

"Hey, Jeff—I think that's him!" Herschel said, looking through binoculars and pointing to the sky. There was something small and dark far away in the gray sky. At first, the small, dark thing looked a lot like a mosquito. Rapidly, it grew. It was the size of a fly. Then a bird. It was coming nearer.

"The big man his own self," Jeffrey said.

Soon after Herschel, Jeffrey, and hundreds of thousands of other people wearing lime-green identified the President's helicopter, the helicopter was right above them. They watched it hover there, wondering what it would do next.

And then they watched it drop, drop, drop.

And vanish from sight.

"It went into the groove!" Herschel exclaimed.

Everyone waited, watching excitedly through binoculars for any sign of what the President was doing in the Grand Canyon-like groove of one of the two largest screws anyone would ever see.

They didn't have to wait long.

Three minutes after the helicopter vanished, it reappeared. People cheered and waved. They waited for the President's instructions. But the helicopter floated higher and higher. It ascended up and away as steadily as a birthday balloon cut loose from the bunch.

"He's not leaving us, is he, Jeff?" Herschel asked, all in one breath.

"Nah, he wouldn't do nothing like that," Jeffrey

reassured him. Yet the same scary question had entered Jeffrey's mind, too. It had entered a lot of people's minds. As the helicopter's propeller tugged the President away from them, it became a very real question: He wasn't going back to the White House, was he?

"Hey! Where you goin'?" someone yelled. "Come back here."

Those in front banged on the chain link fence. They climbed it and shook their fists near the top. The icy wind whipped and whistled around them. All the excitement that had rendered them oblivious to the cold rose up and out of their bodies, chasing after the ascending helicopter.

The national guards removed their guns, anticipating a riot.

"You think he went in there and decided it can't be moved?" Herschel mumbled. He couldn't bear to ask the question any louder.

He watched the President's helicopter move farther and farther away from him. He tried to wish it back, wanting, needing the force of his wish to be greater than the force of the helicopter's propeller. Standing in front of a golden screw that was shinier than anything he'd ever seen, Herschel was more aware than ever that it was sixty-five degrees below zero. He looked behind him and saw nothing but hard, frozen snow—the rumpled white sheet of an unmade bed. The Antarctic wind felt to Herschel like the strings of a tennis racquet, each gust a smashing forehand blow to his face—his chin, cheeks, and nose each taking turns playing the tennis ball. The kind of cold that freezes bones so thoroughly it takes more than an hour in front of a fireplace for them to thaw. He was having a harder time breathing. He pumped his inhaler and sucked in more medicine.

Watching the helicopter leave him behind, and worrying for the first time that he wouldn't be there when Bart's Screw was unscrewed, Herschel nearly had his heart broken. For reasons he didn't understand, Herschel had felt connected to Bart's Screw since he first learned about it, watching the Channel 5 Nightly News with Jeffrey. Something had told him he was supposed to play a hand. He was supposed to be there when it was unscrewed.

Then the helicopter stopped rising. Herschel's heart, barely intact, swelled. He heard a voice.

"MY FELLOW AMERICANS, AND ALL OTHER GREAT PEOPLE OF THIS WORLD," boomed the President over the helicopter's speaker system, "IT IS NOW TIME WE COME TOGETHER AND REMOVE THIS MOST SIGNIFICANT OF DISCOVERIES. IF EVERYONE WOULD PLEASE WALK TOWARD THE CENTER OF THE SCREW."

The national guards removed single keys from lime-green breast pockets and slid them into the padlocks.

"Single file now, y'hear?"

Chapter 20

The plan was simple. Every man and woman and the one child in Antarctica was to climb down one of the tall ladders set up in the screw's groove. This would take some time because the ladders really were tall. Each ladder post consisted of three trunks of California's tallest Redwoods thatched together. Once everyone was safely down a ladder to the floor of the groove, half of them were supposed to push against a half of one side, while the other half pushed against the other half of the other side.

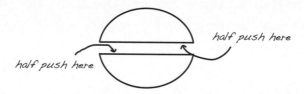

The plan had to work. They'd all come too far not to see Bart's Screw unscrewed.

After several hours of waiting in lines and tiptoeing

nervously down ladders, the cold, tired, hungry men, women, and (one) child at the South Pole were handed bag lunches, compliments of the United States government. They pulled blankets out of their backpacks and sat down to eat lunch—a picnic in the Antarctic. If you've ever been camping with your family, you know that after being without food for a long time and doing something so rigorous it drains you of all your energy, almost anything tastes delicious. That said, nobody complained about the bag lunches they'd been handed as they stepped off the ladders. To Herschel, his bologna sandwich and hot cocoa in a Styrofoam cup were ambrosia: a meal fit for the gods.

"Whatcha eatin, Jeffrey?" he asked, tasting the salty meat on his lips. He pumped his inhaler and sucked in the medicine, trying to catch his breath after climbing down a seven-hundred-foot tall ladder.

"Same's you. Same's everybody else. We all got the same thing."

"It's good, huh?"

"Not bad. Just wish there was more of it."

"Me, too. 'Least it's not so cold down here."

One thing nice about picnicking at the bottom of the groove was that it was a lot warmer than up on top of the screw. The high gold walls provided complete protection from the wind. Sure the gold was cold, but the blankets Herschel and all the others sat on kept them warm. Bartholomew Rogers' advice proved helpful once again. The second of his Three Important (and Simple!)

Things to Remember for Antarctic Survival was

**Bring blankets. Lots of blankets.
You never know when you'll need them.**

Everyone ate quickly because they were hungry and because they were ready to give the President's plan a try. Herschel pumped his inhaler once again and sucked in the medicine before standing with his brother and a huge mass of people set to push one quarter of the screw.

"You think it's gonna to work?" he asked.

"Don't see why not. Seems logical. We'll be doing the same thing as a screwdriver," his big brother answered.

"Yeah, guess so. Seems awful big, though, you know."

"Good thing you don't got to unscrew it all by yourself." Jeffrey smiled at his twelve-year-old brother, so eager to help.

Officially, no person younger than eighteen had been permitted to make the trip to the South Pole. But Herschel had prepared to go anyway. He'd spent the whole month before the trip guessing what it was they were going to find underneath the screw: "You think it plugs up a volcano?" he'd asked. "Or maybe we find a couple giant hamsters—you know, they make the world spin when they run? Hey, what if nothin's underneath it? Guess that'd be funny, though. Everyone cares so much, kinda be funny if all the fuss was over nothin'." And yet, despite his sense of humor, Herschel cared more than anyone. It didn't matter how many times Jeffrey told his little brother he was too young and that he couldn't go; Herschel was set on being there when Bart's Screw was unscrewed.

Really, Herschel didn't know why he cared so much. Something, maybe the screw itself, had beckoned to him, insisting he be at the South Pole when they unscrewed Big Bart. He'd begged Jeffrey to make the trip, even without him, so he could return home and tell Herschel all about it. And then he'd convinced Jeffrey to let him walk along to the boarding dock so he could, " 'least say good-bye."

Minutes before the last boat to Antarctica drifted away from the North Carolina shore, Herschel had jammed himself between two large adults in a boarding line. A deckhand taking tickets at the entrance spotted Herschel when he got to the front of the line and asked for his ID. With a frown, the deckhand had told Herschel, "Sorry, mate, yer a wee bit too young." But after Herschel pleaded with him for fifteen minutes, even delaying the boat's departure, the deckhand had finally conceded. "Right, mate, run along. You make yourself of use, now, y'hear?"

Now, in the groove of the screw Herschel had been so determined to get to, Jeffrey said to his brother, "I don't doubt you could move it all by yourself, little bro."

The President's wispy, wind-blown voice interrupted their conversation. From high up in his helicopter, he delivered his instruction.

"OKAY, EVERYONE . . . READY? . . . PUSH!"

And push they did. All three-hundred-some thousand

people in the groove of Bart's screw pushed. But nothing happened. The screw didn't move even the tiniest, most microscopic fraction of a centimeter. They pushed again, and again the screw wouldn't budge. After over three minutes and multiple fruitless attempts, people stopped pushing, exhausted. The grumbling began.

"It's too heavy," someone said.

"It can't be moved," added another.

"It was a stupid idea in the first place," agreed a third person.

None of these people knew that the screw's weight wasn't the problem. Collectively, they had enough muscle to unscrew it. The problem was that years and years of sitting underneath Antarctica's snow and ice had frozen the screw to the ground. Once the seal of ice around it was broken, the screw would rotate easily enough.

"I KNOW YOU'RE TIRED. I KNOW YOU'RE FRUSTRATED," said the President, "BUT WE OWE IT TO OURSELVES AND TO EVERYONE WHO COULDN'T BE HERE TODAY TO GIVE IT ONE MORE SHOT. ARE YOU WITH ME?"

Not everybody agreed enthusiastically, but a general "Why not? What do we have to lose?" feeling trickled through the crowd. With their hands flat against the gold wall in front of them, the desperate mass of people at the South Pole waited for the President's go-ahead.

"READY . . . PUSH!"

Again, nothing happened. The screw simply would not move. Bent at their waists with their arms straight in front of them and their chins touching their chests, the grown men and women in the groove of Bart's Screw looked like hundreds of thousands of six-year-olds struggling with too-big family lawn mowers.

The screw just wasn't unscrewing.

Herschel stepped back and watched the straining faces of all the intrepid citizens of the world who had traveled thousands of miles to the coldest spot on the planet to see something it now appeared they weren't going to see.

Herschel was mad. Mad at himself for not being stronger. Mad at the President because his plan hadn't worked. Mad at the golden screw that wouldn't budge. That had broken so many people's hearts. Yes, Herschel was mad at the screw. Livid. He pumped his inhaler, closed his eyes, and breathed in the medicine. Rage surged through him. He couldn't take it anymore.

"Aaaaaaaaaaahhh!" he screamed. He ran toward the wall, leapt into the air, and kicked it with both feet. He landed on his back.

Crrrrrrrrrrrrrrraaaaaaaaaaaaaaaack.

That's all it took. That one extra kick from the smallest person at the South Pole was all it took to break the seal of ice around a screw bigger than any screw anyone had ever begun to imagine. Herschel's kick started a crack that wended its way loudly around the screw.

When ice cracks, it makes two sounds simultaneously: a hissing, sibilant sound, like your local librarian's shush when she puts her finger to her lips, telling you to keep the noise down; and a crescendoing series of popping sounds, like a bag of Orville Redenbacher's in the microwave. It was these two joyous sounds—distinguishable yet merging into one—that each person in the groove heard at a different time, as the crack raced jaggedly around Bart's Screw.

They were the sounds Herschel, everyone in Antarctica, and everyone else around the world who wanted to be there but couldn't had been waiting and working and hoping and praying for. The sounds of the seal cracking and the screw moving ever so slightly invigorated and inspired. Every man, every woman, and the one child in the groove was stunned to elation and stopped pushing to admire their accomplishment, shake hands, hug, and jump for joy.

"KEEP PUSHING!" the President's voice ordered.

They pushed. And the screw moved. First it rotated four inches. Then four feet. Then fourteen feet. The screw spun and spun. You may have experienced this yourself if you've ever used a screwdriver or tried to open a pickle jar. When the screw or cap has been screwed tight, the hardest part of unscrewing it comes initially; after you get the screw or cap moving, your job gets easier.

As they unscrewed Bart's Screw, it rose out of the ground. The head of the screw—with the hundreds of thousands of people clad in lime-green toiling in its groove—spun higher and higher and higher.

No one bothered to look down.

Chapter 21

Inventory

What you know about Calvin Comet Cobble at this point in our story:

- He's twelve.
- He's an orphan who lives in cereal box-shaped orphanage on an island that is actually the core (or pit) of the planet Earth.
- He's got the biggest, brightest, wildest shock of red-orange hair anyone who's met him has ever seen. Hidden Shores orphans and teachers think it looks like his head is on fire and that his freckles look like smoldering embers.
- He's seen a girl swallowed up by the Shadow, and she was never spit back out. Cal watched Belinda hesitantly step into the Shadow and—Poof!—disappear. He witnessed her final moments in the lighted world. He did nothing to stop her. He shouted in his head but not out loud.
- He's lonely.

- He has one friend at Hidden Shores; her name is Berneatha Twiggins, and she's seven.
  - ° He may have just made another.
- Cal's mother—a wonderful woman—died of heartbreak shortly after she gave birth to Cal. She died because half of her heart was so happy and the other half was so sad, and her heart just couldn't survive the tug of war. She was happy because she had a beautiful, healthy new son, Calvin Comet Cobble. She was sad because her husband wasn't there with her and because he would never meet their son.
- Cal doesn't know who his father is. He doesn't know why he's never met him.
- He was sent to an orphanage in Detroit when he was three days old.
- He was transferred to a brand new orphanage called Hidden Shores when he was five years old because the orphanage in Detroit was filling up and nobody had shown any interest in adopting an orphan with wild red hair and the last name Cobble. "Now there's a little troublemaker," four-year-old Cal had overheard one potential adopter saying to his wife. "He'll be in jail before he can vote. They told me he's Ronald Cobble's son. Didn't his father have red hair as well?"
- Cal doesn't think his red-orange hair looks like fire. He thinks it looks like red-orange hair.
- He has never skipped a stone.

Chapter 22

This Very Year
(Twelve Years After Unscrewing Bart's Screw)

Cal's breakfast tasted better than ever that morning. There was nothing special or even different about the cheetah-cake he nibbled on as he walked in line around the cafeteria; it was the same rock hard yet squirmy "fruit and protein" egg dish he and the rest of Hidden Shores orphans had eaten for the past one year, two months, and seven days. Cal's mind was just on other things. He kept thinking about Mr. Englewood. Kept hearing his stone skipping whisperingly across Lake Arctic.

"What in the world are you smiling about, Calvin Cobble?" Cal looked up from his tray and his thoughts to see Berneatha walking next to him, working hard to keep up with her short legs and large feet. "We almost get busted this morning, and now you're eating eggs and raisins cooked to slimy perfection. In a few minutes, we're gonna be sitting in Miss Truly Annoying's classroom. So you tell me: what's there to smile about?"

"Ah. Hey, Bernie. I was just thinking . . . anyway, we're supposed to be walking single-file, right? Don't you ever follow the rules?"

Now it was Berneatha's turn to smile: "When they suit me."

Cal's smile expanded into a big, happy grin. He couldn't be irritated with his pig-tailed friend for very long. She had too much confidence. Confidence that he admired and wished he shared.

"I was just thinking about this morning," Cal said. "We got ourselves out of some serious trouble, huh?"

"Oh yeah. If Principal Warden had found us, we'd probably be digging our own graves in the Shadow. Trying to not bump into each other." (She pronounced "Warden" as "Wahden.")

"I'd dig yours if you'd dig mine."

The two friends were letting go of a whole day's mutual frustration.

"That way it wouldn't be so hard," Berneatha said. "I wouldn't be worried about spending the rest of eternity choking on the same soil I was digging up. I'd just be doing the world a favor by getting rid of you."

The hand not balancing her tray was on her hip again, but her banter was playful now instead of lecturing.

Cal laughed. "I'd be digging and thinking how I wasn't gonna have to put up with you ever again."

"No more having to save your life all the time, Calvin Cobble."

"And no more interrogations."

"Ooh. Fancy word for a twelve-year-old: 'interrogations.' " Berneatha, off-the-charts-smart and proud of it, took her time saying "interrogations," pronouncing her R sound mockingly. She added: "No more helping you with your homework."

"No more babysitting."

Smiling and laughing and joyfully insulting each other.

"No more putting up with your lies."

"No more being followed around like a shadow all the time."

"No more disobeying the rules and walking side-by-side in the cafeteria."

Gulp.

Neither Cal nor Berneatha had said it. They turned at the same time to look behind them. Standing there was a full-grown man in a rumpled suit—his arms crossed, his thinning hair parted to the side in front of his red bald spot, his mouth squeezed into a wry, sly smile.

Principal Warden.

Chapter 23

Principal Warden had a violent, volcanic temper and a megaphonic voice.

Fifteen-year-olds on the twelfth floor claimed they could hear him scolding a student all the way down in his office. He'd been known to throw young orphans out of first- and second-floor windows and to break meter sticks over older students' heads in fits of rage. If Principal Warden was mad and you were in his line of sight, there was a good chance you or at least your eardrums were going to be injured.

And once he was mad, there was no reasoning with him. Orphans learned not to plead their cases or even cry before him. He called it all "talking back," and there was nothing that he found more disrespectful or infuriating than an orphan "talking back." Every plea and every tear was like a drop of gasoline on the fire of his rage. He just got madder and madder and madder.

Hidden Shores orphans had but one solid defense against their Principal's wrath: forewarning.

When Principal Warden is mad at you, you know it before he opens his mouth. The principal and headmaster of Hidden Shores Orphanage has a bald spot on the top of his head that expands every year. When he gets mad, the bald spot inevitably turns as red as molten lava oozing down a mountain.

When he erupts, your only chance in the world is to run! run! run! run! run! To pick up and move to a safer place, leaving your belongings and self-confidence and whatever else you have with you behind.

Of course when you live in an orphanage at the center of the Earth, there aren't many options for relocation.

Sitting in the principal's office, Cal found himself staring at the man in charge's molten-red bald spot.

"Have either of you an explanation for your recalcitrance?" Principal Warden asked. His tone controlled but combustible.

"Uh . . . our recal—recal—sir?" stuttered Cal.

"He means why weren't we following the rules," Berneatha said.

"Yes. That is exactly what I mean, Miss Twiggins."

Berneatha said, "We were just talking and got a little excited, Principal Warden. It really isn't that big a deal."

Cal once again admired his friend's courage. He knew that, in spite of himself, he would let her do all the talking. He checked himself out of the conversation.

It was out of his control.

Cal looked around Principal Warden's office. Really, there wasn't much to look at. The floor was dark wood, the walls were white and undecorated plaster—except for a map of Robert tacked next to a knotty wood frame hanging crooked on a nail and displaying the principal's diploma, which confirmed his advanced degree in education. The degree was from Dragoona University. Cal didn't know where Dragoona University was, but he always thought the diploma looked very important and official. Every time Cal was in the principal's office, however, he also noticed something odd about the diploma. It had been awarded to "Principal Warden"; as if Principal Warden had no first name; or maybe his first name was, actually, Principal, and he'd been destined for his current job since shortly after birth.

Cal shuddered at the idea.

He looked back at the principal, who sat behind his wide oak desk. There was a two-foot-tall, very lifelike nickel bust of the principal on the desk. His sharp nose, his thin lips, his intense glare, and even his bald spot were there. The nickel at the bust's bald spot had even started to turn red with age. You could tell the bust had been done a couple years earlier because its bald spot wasn't as wide as the principal's was now.

Principal Warden was looking, for the moment, at Berneatha. The bust was keeping an eye on Cal. Cal took a deep breath. Being stared at by an angry nickel head was creepy, but he'd take it over being stared at by an angry in-the-flesh Principal Warden any day.

The principal was listening to Berneatha say, "Geez. We were just talking. We weren't getting into any trouble. I don't mean to be rude, Principal Warden, but this is a waste of time." His bald spot was so red it could have led Santa's sleigh through a blizzard. His lips were pursed tight and trembling, as if words of remonstration were ramming them from inside his mouth, trying to escape. His hands were tense on the desk in front of him. He looked to Cal like he was ready to pounce from his chair and end their discussion. Maybe end their lives.

Berneatha continued: "Principal Warden, if you don't mind my asking, are you gonna punish us or not? I'm not telling you how to do your job; it's just we should be in class right now, if you ask me. Not that that's a place of learning, either."

The principal rose out of his chair a couple inches. Cal thought, *Berneatha's gonna get us both killed*. But it wasn't Berneatha who finally triggered the eruption.

Cal realized something, sitting there in Principal Warden's office, looking into a fierce nickel mien and awaiting his punishment: It was the first time he'd been in this office when his reason for being there had nothing to do with his hair. He was in the office this time because he'd actually broken a rule.

The thought made him smile.

That did it.

"Do you think this is funny, young man?" Principal Warden bolted upright, becoming an upside-down exclamation point, illustrating his anger. "Am I funny to you?

Are my rules funny?" He was pointing his finger now, all of his anger directed at Cal. "You—with that provocative red hair—you provoked this disobedience! I'll tell you what's funny, you little rabble-rouser. I told them when I took you in, 'Like father, like son!' The next time you break one of my rules, I'll let you think about it good and long on the left side of the island. How funny will that be, young man? I bet some of the fine fellows at Robert Penitentiary will be happy to wipe that smile off your face for you."

The principal was shaking with anger. Too angry, it appeared, to think of a proper punishment for the cheeky little girl and the redheaded punk troublemaker. Too angry to think at all. Finally, he managed: "Get out of my office! Both of you."

Then he picked up his bust and threw it, as if it were a dodgeball, at the orphans. The bust—bald spot leading the way—just missed Cal's head, torpedoing into the white plaster wall behind him, denting the wall before falling to the floor.

That wall could have been my head, Cal thought. His head had nearly been dented by the bald spot of a nickel bust.

Cal stood there, stunned to stillness. *What did he mean,* Like father, like son?

"C'mon," he heard Berneatha say. And then he was yanked out of the office and into the cafeteria.

Chapter 24

Where have you been? Young man? Young lady?" Miss Trudy stood in front of Cal and Berneatha. She patted her bouffant hair and tugged on her fuchsia flower-print dress where it bunched at her waist. "And to think I had given you the benefit of the doubt and assumed that you, young man, were combing your hair and that you, young lady, were helping him." She looked past them to the rest of the class, sighed, gestured theatrically, and said, "Helping us all."

"Why would I help him comb his hair?" Berneatha said, trudging by Miss Trudy to her desk.

Cal began to mutter, "I'm sorr—" but stopped, not willing to apologize as he had every other day for six years, and simply walked by the patting and tugging teacher to his desk.

Miss Trudy collected herself enough to say, "If you two disrupt the class once more today, I will have to send you to Principal Warden's office."

She looked satisfied.

"We just came from Principal Warden's office," Berneatha said.

Surprised into further patting and tugging, Miss Trudy finally sputtered, "Well, good, then, that is surely where you belong. I am positive that the next time he will send you out to the left side of the island."

Berneatha rolled her eyes.

"I'll tell my dad you're coming," Hector said, smirking. "He's over there, you know." He said this last part not just to Cal and Berneatha but to the whole class.

"Yeah, we've heard," Cal muttered to himself. He was sick of Hector always talking about his dad. It reminded Cal of his own dad—the missing man. The man who had left him before he was even born.

"What was that, Torch?"

"Nothing, Hector." Cal didn't look back to face the bully. "I was just talking to myself."

"That's right. You bettera been just talking to yourself. When my dad escapes I'll tell him to get you first. I'll tell him he can find you in the dark. Torchy freak." Hector shoved Cal in the back of the head so hard Cal's forehead slammed into his desk. When Cal rolled back up into a sitting position, forehead crimson and smarting, Hector shoved the back of his head again. This time Cal's nose hit his desk. When he rolled back up again, his nose was bleeding.

Hector laughed and pointed. "Oh no, the fire's

spreading. Someone call the fire department."

Cal looked around the room. He didn't see any tissues. He tore a small piece of paper from his notebook and crunched it up his gushing nostril.

Hector feigned caution. "Don't feed the fire with paper. It'll just make it spread faster," he said.

As had become the tradition in Miss Trudy's classroom, everyone stared at Cal.

"The blood's almost the same color as his hair," Joe said.

"At least it matches. We wouldn't want to clash," added giggling Cicely.

"He still looks like an alien," Corretta said.

"I can't see," complained Mason from the floor.

"That is enough. Enough. I absolutely do not know how we will ever recover from this disruption." Miss Trudy patted her hair and tugged on her fuchsia flower-print dress. "One more word out of any of you for the rest of the day, and you will have a conversation with Principal Warden. I believe you can thank two of your classmates for already having his temper preheated." The room silenced. The orphans sat up a little straighter. "Menaces, all of you. Hmm. I would like to have a word with whoever it is that raised you barnyard animals."

You did, Cal thought. You *raised us*. Indeed, Miss Trudy had been the only adult consistently present in the last six years of most of her students' lives. But he didn't dare tell her that. Just as he didn't dare tell her that he could taste blood on his upper lip, where it had run to from his injured nose (notebook paper is too stiff to effectively seal a nostril), and he didn't dare ask her if he could go to the bathroom and clean his face. He'd already survived one encounter and one almost-encounter with Principal Warden today. He didn't want to push his luck. His reward for staying out of trouble, he reminded himself, was the chance to skip a stone with Mr. Englewood.

Chapter 25

Bart's Screw kept rotating and rising. People in the groove now jogged as they pushed. For many miles the work got easier and easier. They reached the President's helicopter and kept going, leaving it well below.

It is rather incredible that these men and women and (one) child moved such a large object without tiring. But it is not the display of each individual's strength and endurance that makes what happened that day such an unprecedented act. There have been accounts of impossible, heroic deeds recorded throughout human history. People have done incredible things with adrenaline rushing through their bodies. Parents have lifted cars off their children. Campers have ripped off sleeping bags upon hearing bears in their campsites. An Athenian man named Philippides once even sprinted twenty-six miles from Marathon back to Athens to announce victory in a battle with the Persians and to warn his fellow citizens of impending attack. What separates the adrenaline rush at the South Pole that day from all those other phenomenal feats is the teamwork involved—the number of people inspired to accomplish the same goal.

They pushed Bart for four days, taking shifts, eating bologna sandwiches and drinking hot chocolate on their brief breaks. When the head of the screw entered the clouds, the fog was so thick no one in the groove could see even as far as the wall they were pushing. But they kept jogging, and they kept pushing.

Then the head of the screw came out of the clouds and spun so high breathing became difficult. The work got harder and harder.

"How . . . much . . . higher . . . Jeff?" Herschel wheezed. His asthma made breathing almost impossible miles above the mainland.

"Not too much, Hersch. Hang in there, pal."

He heard Jeffrey's words of encouragement. Then he fell. Fainted, that is, right into his big brother's arms. Before he passed out, he mumbled, "Whatta . . . ya . . . think's . . . under it?"

Jeffrey unzipped Herschel's coat pocket and found his inhaler. He jabbed it into Herschel's mouth and pumped. Nothing came out. He brought it up to his ear and shook it. Empty. "No!" he screamed, hurling the inhaler down the groove.

"How we gonna get you down from here, Hersch," Jeffrey said. His brother needed air.

The head of the screw rose toward the end of Earth's

atmosphere. The conditions were quickly becoming dangerous. Several other people in the groove fainted.

Bart's Screw wobbled.

People in the groove stopped pushing just in time. The bottom tip of the screw was all that remained to unscrew.

On its tip, Big Bart listed side to side like a sailboat in choppy waters. People began to panic. The President's voice was faint. To those hundreds of thousands of brave souls miles above, his voice was only a whisper.

"Hold tight," said the soft voice. "Help is on the way."

"We don't got time to hold tight, Hersch," Jeffrey said. He unzipped his jacket and peeled it off, then tied it around his waist. His brother in his arms, he ran hundreds of yards, zigzagging and dodging hugging and praying citizens, never stopping to catch his breath, to the opening at the end of the groove.

He looked down and saw only clouds below him. He closed his eyes tight, took a deep breath, and swallowed back the dizziness he felt coming on. He waited as the screw leaned back, back, back. Before it came forward again, he jumped.

Jumped right off the head of the screw.

Chapter 26

This Very Year
(Twelve Years After Unscrewing Bart's Screw)

Slipping out the front door of Hidden Shores Orphan-age, his forehead and nose still stinging from the previous morning, Cal had to convince himself not to scamper over to Aunt Robbie and climb up into her familiar branches. As he passed the marvelous tree and made his way across the grand front lawn, immaculately cut, he wondered if Mr. Englewood remembered inviting him back. Would he be annoyed that he had to share the beach once again? Would Cal even be able to skip a rock, anyway? He didn't have a ropey arm or strong springy legs like Mr. Englewood. He didn't want to embarrass himself and waste his teacher's time.

And walking next to the Shadow, he always felt uneasy.

But he wasn't only feeling uneasy. He was feeling something else, too, something he couldn't identify right then.

He was feeling excited.

It had been a long, long time since he'd been genuinely excited. Even that first morning he'd spotted Mr. Englewood through his bedroom window, he hadn't been truly excited. He'd been curious—even intrigued—but not excited. To be excited you have to have hope for something better. For you to be excited to go to school in the morning, for instance, it may need to be Field Day, when you know you'll get to run in races, ride your bike, and eat ice cream instead of doing schoolwork. Cal—dropped in a helicopter onto a place he didn't care for and that didn't care for him (they certainly did not have Field Day at Hidden Shores), and with a big lake, a dangerous, dark Shadow, and Earth's Mantle between him and any other, happier place—well, Cal had stopped hoping for anything better a long time ago.

It had been so long since he'd been genuinely excited that not only could he not identify the feeling at first, but he didn't know what to do with it once he did. He'd been too excited to sleep all night. Staring at the nearly full moon passing by the hole in Earth's crust and mantle, he kept thinking how it looked like a skipping stone itself, round and flat. He wondered: if you could find someone big and strong enough to do it, not to mention a big enough body of water, would the moon skip? He knew it really wasn't flat, but . . .

"Well, well. Look what the cat dragged in." Mr. Englewood looked Cal up and down. His eyes smiled as he examined the top of Cal's head. "That cat must have grabbed hold of your hair before he started dragging."

Cal's neighbor stood tall as ever, blocking the sun so that all Cal could see was the dark mantle behind him. He extended his hand, and Cal took it, their second handshake coming on the second day of their acquaintance.

"What do you say, Cal Cobble. How 'bout we find you a stone?"

Cal nodded. "Flat and round," he said. He grinned with his teacher as they began to pace, together.

"That's it," Mr. Englewood said.

"But not too big or too small," Cal said.

"Now you're talking."

They walked a few paces, Mr. Englewood already picking up, dropping, picking up, dropping. His purple tie swung side-to-side behind him like a pendulum. Mr. Englewood looked behind him and saw Cal's eyes following the tie. "It's for balance, Cal. More superstitious than anything, I'm sure, but it seems to me if you're trying to throw something straight, throw it so it doesn't jump or dive or arc, you want some sense of balance, something happening in the opposite direction, too." Mr. Englewood laughed at his own logic and returned his focus to the rock beach.

After a time, Cal picked up a stone. "How about this one, Mr. Englewood?" he asked, his nerves and worry giving way to hope. This could be the day he skipped one, just like Mr. Englewood.

"Now that, Cal Cobble, I can't tell you. Once you know the guidelines, you got to pick your own stone."

He continued to look down at the rocks as he spoke, his concentration too focused to be compromised by conversation. "Every hand and every stone's different. You trying to find a match. Fittin' 'em together like puzzle pieces. Only you gonna know what feels just right.

"And you will, too. You'll know it when you find it."

They paced some more, Cal hustling to keep up with Mr. Englewood, whose stride you couldn't measure with a yardstick.

The whole beach was made up of relatively flat rocks, and Cal had trouble distinguishing one from another. He bent over and picked one up. It was flat and round and seemed, from his limited experience, like a good stone to skip. But when he moved it between his pointer-finger and thumb, he had to stretch them almost straight to hold it. He guessed that meant it was too big, that it didn't feel just right. He dropped it and moved on.

The next stone he picked up didn't make him stretch his pointer finger and thumb, but it had a sharp point on its edge that pricked his hand. He dropped it and moved on.

He picked up another, dropped it, and moved on. And another. And another. He dropped each one and moved on.

Mr. Englewood pivoted and walked back in the opposite direction. Cal pivoted, too, keeping up, taking two strides for every one of his teacher's. Mr. Englewood already had four stones in his hand.

Then Cal saw it.

A white stone, round and flat, of course, appearing almost astral, partially buried under several purplish stones.

He bent over and picked it up. The stone seemed to move itself between his thumb and pointer-finger, the curve of its edge matching precisely the curve of his hand. Everything—Lake Arctic lapping up on Bob's shore, his own weight crunching the rocks beneath him, and Mr. Englewood's soft barefooted steps—went silent as he examined the stone. It was small, Cal thought, maybe three inches long and two wide, and almost a circle—the edge on one side straight instead of curved. Now that he thought about it, the stone looked like the moon he'd stared at the night before: white with silvery blotches and not quite full. But the stone, unlike the moon, really was flat. A skippable moon, it was. Cal could already imagine this miniature moon bounding boldly across Lake Arctic like one of the stones Mr. Englewood threw.

"Mr. Englewood, I—I've got it," he said.

Mr. Englewood looked up, finally, from the rocks, first at Cal's hand and then into his eyes. He took a deep breath. "Oh, my. And there it is. You found it now, didn't you?"

Cal was so excited his ears buzzed. "Can I skip it?"

Mr. Englewood stood there not talking for a moment. Then he said, "No, Cal, you're not gonna skip that one. Not today." He said it with certainty that surprised Cal.

Cal's heart dropped into his stomach. Mr. Englewood wasn't going to let him skip his stone. Suddenly, oddly, without warning, he got angry. Calvin Comet Cobble got angry. "But you said—you said I could skip one today, Mr. Englewood! You said I could." And then: "No one lets me do anything I wanna do." He sounded selfish and ridiculous, he knew, but he couldn't help it. Anger rushed up and out of him now, as if it had been locked up for years, chained by the leg to Excitement in some dark, damp dungeon in his chest, never to be seen again. Cal had met Mr. Englewood then, and Excitement finally escaped, squeezing through cell bars and running up the dungeon stairs to freedom. It was Anger's turn to speak. "My parents leave me, I get sent down here to this—this place!—and I have no say. Everyone looks, I mean, *stares* at me. Because my hair's red? And—and I can't even ask questions! All of it. It's all out of my control!" Cal's voice was getting louder and louder. He was ready to shout— he didn't care if he woke up everyone at Hidden Shores, not even Principal Warden. "Why! Why can't I skip it!" Declaring and not asking, talking more to the world— inside and outside—than to Mr. Englewood or anyone else. The bridge of his nose tingled, his face twitched, and he did something he'd never done in the six years he'd lived inside Earth.

He cried.

First two tears, one from each eye, then more. And still more. Too many to count. He couldn't stop crying. He didn't want to. The crying felt good; it made his head light, his face hot and puffy. There was pressure at his temples, and his face felt bloated, as if his head was a full water cooler, his eyes the spigots.

He kept saying "Why!" as he cried, a "Why!" for every tear. Kept repeating it over and over. Why? Why? Why? Why?

And then there was a hand on his shoulder.

A voice there with him: "Whoa. Easy now."

But having Mr. Englewood's hand on his shoulder just made Cal want to keep crying, for different reasons. His breaths and tears became sobs. Deep sobs. Sobs of sadness, abandonment, defeat, and now, miraculously, hope—all blended together.

Cal looked up through blurry eyes at Mr. Englewood; Mr. Englewood looked down to Cal, confused but understanding.

"Just you take it easy, Cal." His hand steady on Cal's shoulder. "You're not gonna skip that one today, but you're gonna skip another one."

Cal gulped back tears. "But. This one's perfect, Mr. Englewood. I know it."

"Yeah, you're right. It's perfect. I can tell by the way you looking at it, the way you holding it. That's why you're not gonna skip it, not today."

Cal's eyes were clearing, though he still felt tears on his face. His stomach was suddenly empty, like he hadn't eaten in days. He asked, "But why not?"

"Because Cal, you care too much about that stone. Means too much to you. That's one you wanna hold on to, throw it when you really ready to let it go."

Mr. Englewood said, "You find a safe place for that

stone. You'll find another one to skip today, trust me."

Cal wanted to make a run for the lake, to throw his stone because it was his and he could throw it whenever he wanted to. He knew that Mr. Englewood wouldn't stop him. But something told him to trust his new friend. Trust that he was sincere, that he cared. Cal looked into his new teacher's eyes and carefully dropped the stone into the right front pocket of his jeans. He wiped tears from his face with the back of his hand. "Okay, Mr. Englewood. Can we keep looking?"

Mr. Englewood grinned again. "Let's do that."

Now that he knew what he was looking for, it didn't take Cal long to find a purplish stone that felt just right. Despite being the same approximate size, shape, and weight, it didn't feel as good—as perfect—between his pointer-finger and thumb as the white, dimpled stone now in his pocket, but it matched his hand fine. It would do.

"You ready to go?" Mr. Englewood asked.

"Yeah. Got it." Cal showed him the stone.

"How 'bout you go make that thing a bunny? Let it hop around out there, sniffin for cabbage."

Cal laughed at the analogy. He was feeling excited and hopeful again, his breath catching and his heart racing.

It's going to happen, he thought. *I'm really going to skip a stone. Or at least throw a stone at the water.*

They walked up to the water together. They turned and faced each other. "Remember what I said yesterday, now, huh? Dig your feet in." They both dug their feet in.

"Bend your knees." They bent their knees. "Shift your weight on over to your back foot." They did this so that only the toes of their front feet were touching the rock beach. "Now let your arm swing back and up and give it all you got when you bring it back down. Don't fight your body."

Cal swung his arm back and brought it forward as hard as he could.

He let go of his stone.

Cal's stone didn't whiz through the air like the stones Mr. Englewood threw. It didn't travel in the same persistent horizontal plane.

Cal's stone dove down to the water, meeting it about fifteen feet from shore.

Cal had only enough time to think, *Oh, no, it'll sink.* Miraculously, however, gloriously, it did not sink. It hit the water and bounced up, almost straight up, and then fell back down just outside the ring in the water it had caused.

Cal's stone had skipped. Once.

"Well, would you look at that. You're a natural, Cal Cobble. You skipped a stone on your first try."

Chapter 27

Principal Warden had called for an after-lunch all-school assembly.

The orphans sat smooshed together on the hard tile floor of the cafeteria, facing the kitchen doors. In front of the doors sat their teachers in plush, comfy, maroon chairs, facing the orphans. There were ten of them, all together. From left to right:

Ms. Querk, who currently taught kindergarten, and who never wore matching shoes. Today she was wearing a flip-flop sandal on her right foot and a steel-toed work boot on her left.

Bespectacled and greasy-haired Mr. Leonine Locks, who stuttered and insisted that his first-grade students call him Leo. They'd locked him in the classroom closet four times that year already.

Miss Ohnsonjay, second grade, who spoke exclusively in Pig Latin and insisted that her students do the same.

Mr. Amradio, third grade, who never changed the volume or pitch of his voice. It was hard to know when he was telling you something and when he was asking you a question.

Miss Ecklebreck, who repeated the same math lesson every day. Her fourth-graders were perhaps the world's best multipliers by nine. (Though they weren't very good at multiplying by eight or eleven.)

Miss Pritzle, fifth grade, who refereed Hidden Shores Orphanage's annual thumb war tournament. (Every orphan in the building participated in the thumb war tournament. The winner of the single-elimination contest got second helpings of the next day's lunch.) She considered herself an authority on the sport, since she herself had never lost a thumb war. She'd also never engaged in a thumb war.

Miss Trudy, whom you've already met.

Mr. Hoot, who seemed to have eyes in the back of his head. He wore shaded glasses with reflective mirrors on the sides, and he could write on the board and keep an eye on his class at the same time.

Pale-skinned Miss Tudor, who didn't like boys. They simply had too much energy, she said, and their attention spans were too short. For their sakes, she pretended her boy students were girls. She called John Walker Joan Walker and Carl Eddleson Carla Eddleson.

And finally, Mr. Bruno, the phys ed teacher, to whom you were previously introduced. He keeps a sleeping bag behind the orphanage and cooks his own meals over a small fire he builds and extinguishes each day.

An uncomplicated man, that Mr. Bruno.

Before the first physical education class of the day, he tapes a sign to the front door so it can be seen from outside the orphanage. The sign says,

Do not tackle.

Do not giggle. (You may laugh, chortle, titter, or snigger, but you may not, under any circumstances, giggle.)

Do not go near the water. Do not, under any circumstances go near the Shadow. Never, ever.

Do not disturb the teacher.

After posting his sign, Mr. Bruno spends the rest of the day sitting on the front steps, rolling and smoking his own cigarettes, and reading Louis L'Amour's *Education of a Wandering Man*. Every day, same routine: sign, smokes, book. He wears a red and black flannel shirt, sleeves rolled up to his elbows, blue jeans, and a worn Brooklyn Dodgers baseball cap with dusty finger prints on the brim. He is always a day unshaven. Despite rarely speaking, he never has a problem with discipline. When the orphans roughhouse or, heaven forbid, giggle, Mr. Bruno looks up from his book, stares the offending orphan(s) down, and exhales two streams of cigarette smoke through his nostrils.

That's all it takes.

There was a portable oak lectern between the orphans and the teachers. Standing at the lectern was Principal Warden.

All eyes were on the principal.

The room was so quiet you could have heard a hair drop from your head to the tile floor.

"Silence!" Principal Warden ordered, pounding a hammer he used as a gavel on the lectern. "The longer you impudent imps share your scuttlebutt, the longer your poor teachers here will be forced to sit and wait."

A couple of the teachers smiled at their boss from their plush, comfy, maroon chairs, thanking him for his consideration. Miss Trudy proudly patted her bouffant hair, then rose an inch and a half out or her chair and tugged on her yellow flower-print dress.

"Now that I have your attention," the principal continued, "there are a few matters we need to discuss."

Cal, sitting toward the back of the room, knew that to discuss with Principal Warden was to be lectured, warned, and threatened. Cal adjusted his position, trying to get comfortable. Students were pressed against him on all sides. He pulled his knees to his chest, making himself as small as he could.

The principal insisted that the orphans sit as close to the lectern as possible so he didn't have to strain his voice to be heard.

The truth is that no Hidden Shores orphan ever had trouble hearing Principal Warden. Principal Warden's voice was loud enough that he never had private conversations with a student or a teacher. If you were on the same floor—and, often, even if you were a couple floors away—you heard his every word. But who was going to tell him that?

"Topic One: Following the Rules," the principal said, brandishing his pointer finger for the audience.

"Here we go," Berneatha whispered into Cal's ear. Berneatha was sitting behind Cal, as she always did at all-school assemblies. It didn't bother her that his hair blocked her view of the front of the room; whenever Cal apologized, as he did now, she reminded him that she'd "rather not see what was going on up there, anyway." She added, "I wish I didn't have to hear it, either."

"What was that? Did someone say something?" said Principal Warden, his bald spot a shade redder than it had been a moment before. "May I remind you all that speaking at an all-school assembly is"—he grinned his sly, wry grin—"quite relevantly, against the rules. And I will not strain my voice trying to talk over you."

Cal could almost hear Berneatha roll her eyes behind him.

"Perhaps it would help if you all moved closer to the podium." There was a collective groan as orphans tried, impossibly, to push themselves even closer to the podium and each other. "Now," the Principal continued, "there was an incident yesterday morning involving two of you. Two of you who were very much out of line." The sly, wry grin returned; Principal Warden was pleased with his pun. "Literally out of line. I caught two students—two of your classmates—walking side-by-side in the cafeteria at breakfast. Now, I'm not going to name names"—as if the orphans hadn't all been there and seen it for themselves— "but let me just say that one of them, a boy old enough to know better, has very distinguishing, um, North Pole follicles, and the other, a younger, shorter girl, is very cheeky indeed."

Cal felt his face flush as orphans shot flames at him with their eyes. He heard someone say, "Today his hair looks like a wave of fire" (as it had all swooped to the left and then curved back to the right). Others chuckled. Not that Cal blamed them. They were as uncomfortable as he was, sitting there on the tile floor knocking shoulders and knees with those sitting next to them. And it appeared they were all here because of Cal and Berneatha. Cal felt compelled right then to pat his right hip pocket. He needed to know the stone he'd found that morning was still there. Needed to feel it in his palm.

"What's your problem," Berneatha whispered to somebody. "Face the front, why don'tcha?"

"Silence!" The principal pounded his hammer on the lectern. "Not another word out of any of you. Have you no respect for your principal, or at least for those in the back struggling to hear?

"Now. Of course there's an important reason for every rule we have here at Hidden Shores Orphanage. Who can tell me why we walk single file around the cafeteria?"

No one said anything. No one raised a hand. No one moved.

Principal Warden looked around the room, his bald spot brighter by the second, like a burner on the stove. "Well, if no one wants to volunteer the answer, I'll choose someone."

Uh-oh, Cal thought. He was always being chosen. His hair had a way of drawing the chooser's attention. He held tighter to his stone through his jeans.

Cal heard the putt and drone of Mr. Englewood's lawn mower starting up, hundreds of yards away. He looked over his right shoulder at the oak front door across the room, knowing that on the other side of the door there was a tree he could disappear into, a calm lake lapping up on the shore, a beach of rocks to be skipped. And over there, on the other side of the door, was Mr. Englewood, getting ready to mow the same endless lawn he mowed every afternoon. Strange, smiling, stone-skipping Mr. Englewood.

"Mr. Cobble," Principal Warden said, as if through a megaphone, "why do we walk single file around the cafeteria?"

The principal's stare was as focused on Cal as his bust's had been the previous morning in his office. He clenched the podium firmly. It wobbled, supporting him as he angrily shifted his balance from his right hand to his left, from his left hand to his right, concentrating on the red-headed mischief-maker surrounded by orphans.

And of course everyone else was staring at Cal, too.

Cal fumbled. It's not that he didn't know the answer. Principal Warden had reminded him and every other orphan of the rules every Thursday for as long as they'd been at Hidden Shores, pounding the rules into their skulls with his hammer-gavel. But Cal couldn't find the answer right then. Not with so many eyes on him. He tried to think. He tried some more. His brain had become a museum, vast and varied, with too many hallways in too many directions, and he couldn't remember where he'd stored the information he was looking for. The best he could do was, "Ah, I don't know, sir. I mean we just always—we always have, I guess."

"Wrong answer, Mr. Cobble!" Principal Warden's sudden shout was loud enough that from your classroom on the outside of the world you may have mistaken it for distant thunder. The principal shook with rage, a kettle about to bubble over. His hands scrambled over his lectern, by habit searching for something to throw. Through pursed lips he squeezed out the words, "You *wouldn't* know, Mr. Cobble." After three of the longest seconds of Cal's life, the headmaster finally shifted his gaze: "Does anybody else know the answer?"

No one spoke. No one raised a hand. No one moved.

And then a hand shot up. A boy said, "I do, Principal Warden."

It was a voice Cal knew. Still, it took him a second to accept that he had raised his hand. He never raised his hand. Certainly not to talk about following rules.

Principal Warden was surprised, too, but he let it show for only the briefest of moments. "Yes, Mr. Nelson. Why do we walk single file?"

Hector Nelson, orphanage bully, who'd beat up or threatened a majority of the orphans in the room, and who specialized in making life miserable for our protagonist, Cal Cobble, cleared his throat—once, twice—and spoke: "We walk single file because it's better exercise. When we walk single file, we walk closer to the wall so we end up walking farther and burning more calories."

Everyone stared, orphans and teachers alike.

"Well, yes. Yes, indeed. That is absolutely correct, Mr. Nelson." Principal Warden beamed. "Perhaps you could get together with your pal Mr. Cobble after our assembly and remind him."

"Yes, sir. It'd be my pleasureful delight." Hector smirked at Cal, his eyes narrowing.

Cal's eyes were wide open.

Principal Warden's voice: "Mr. Cobble, if you would please meet Mr. Nelson out on the front steps immediately following this assembly. Now, if we could get back to the rules.

"Topic two: Arriving to class on time."

Chapter 28

Twelve Years Ago

"Why do I always have to mess things up?" Ron Cobble asked himself. He was supposed to take Julia out for dinner, but he was running late from work. He was still fifteen miles from home, and traffic was terrible. One minute cars would be humming along, traveling the speed limit or faster, and the next minute they'd be stopped, fender-to-fender with the cars in front of and behind them, caught in the bustle of rush hour. For five-minute periods of time, when traffic was stopped, the road was more like a parking lot than a highway.

Traffic was stopped, and it was a parking lot now.

Ron looked at his watch. 5:53. "Yes!" he said. (He meant "No!" of course.) Their reservation was at 6:15, and he still had to pick up Julia. He wanted to shower and shave, too, but he knew he wouldn't have time. The air conditioner in Ron's car was broken, and he was still in his work clothes: a navy blue suit and tie. The low evening sun was hot coming through the windshield, and he'd already sweated through his shirt at the collar and armpits. He felt like an ant in some devilish boy's science experiment with the sun and a magnifying glass. He took his sweaty hands from the steering wheel and rubbed them on his pants.

Traffic still wasn't moving. Ron took his eyes off the road for a second and snatched his wallet from his back pocket. A five and a couple ones. He'd need more money to eat at Donatello's, the new sit-down Italian restaurant overlooking the Mississippi River. He took out his cell phone to call his wife. The phone was dead; he'd forgotten to plug it in at work, which meant he never heard the harried voice mail his wife had left him: something about great pain, the ambulance being on the way, and that he should meet her at the hospital.

HONK!

The driver of the car behind Ron's let him know traffic was moving. Startled, Ron stepped on the accelerator and quickly caught up with the car in front of him. He saw his bank off the highway to the right and, without checking his blind side, he switched lanes to exit.

HONK!

Ron had cut off a fast-moving car in the right lane. The car had had to swerve to avoid a collision. Ron looked in his rearview mirror and waved apologetically. When his eyes returned to the road, traffic had stopped, and he had to stomp with all his might on the brake pedal so as not to hit the car in front of him. His car tires squealed in anguish as they burned on the hot pavement, forced to come to a skidding stop.

Chapter 29

This Very Year
(Twelve Years After Unscrewing Bart's Screw)

Y ou know you don't have to go out there, Calvin
Cobble. You could just go to class. It's not like Miss
Truly Annoying's gonna notice you're there and send you
back down."

Cal was standing with Berneatha by the front door.

"Thanks, Bernie. But they'd all see me. Them, I
mean." He tilted his head toward their fellow orphans,
standing in a half circle around him and Berneatha and
waiting to see what Cal would do. What's going to
happen next? their body language said. It also said, Fight!
Fight! Fight! Fight! Fight! No self-respecting kid—inside
or outside the world—ever misses a fight between classmates. "And Hector's not gonna forget about it. I can't
stay on the ninth floor forever."

The Hidden Shores teachers, odd bunch that they
were, shuffled by the orphans on their way to the elevator
on the far side of the room. Only Mr. Bruno was missing.

He'd gone to the kitchen to rustle up some grub. For Mr. Bruno, that meant the unwanted leftovers he could roast over his own fire. Mr. Hoot watched the orphans in his reflective mirrors as he boarded the elevator. He said, "You students get to class now."

Miss Ohnsonjay said, "Istenlay otay Mr. Oothey, orphansay."

As the teachers crowded into the tiny elevator, the orphans still hadn't moved.

The elevator door closed.

The crowd of Hidden Shores orphans parted, making way for the other fight participant.

The bully, Hector Nelson.

Hector was an imposing figure. Yes, he was tall: 5'10" and going on 6'10" to his fellow orphans. But mostly, he was thick. His body was mature like a man's. He had wide shoulders, almost no neck, and a soft, protruding belly. His white T-shirt and blue jeans, formerly the property of Mr. Amradio, were dirty and faded, and fit snug to his body. He'd cut off the sleeves of the T-shirt, but yellow stains remained under his armpits, which smelled of fish and sour milk. He wore his dark hair short and flat on the top. He was as menacing as any fourteen-year-old you'll ever meet, boy or beast. And he didn't like Cal. He didn't even tolerate Cal. He was a bull, and on Cal's head he saw red.

"Open the door, Torch. Let's go talk about them rules."

The crowd of orphans squirmed. They were anxious

about the fight. It would be good entertainment, they knew—but they didn't want to see anyone (meaning Cal) killed, either.

"Leave him alone, you lousy lout," Berneatha said, stepping between Cal and Hector. Despite her confidence and wit, however, Berneatha was only seven years old and small even for her age. Hector hardly noticed her as he hip-checked her away and to the floor.

"Open it," he ordered, grabbing Cal's shoulders, lifting him off the ground, and spinning him around.

Cal rotated the doorknob and pulled, opening the door to the bright afternoon. The day's heat rushed to meet him. The same seventy-one degrees of sunny, molten warmth Robertians on the right side of the island experienced every day seemed warmer to Cal today. His feet were sweating. And he could smell Hector's acrid armpits behind him.

Out on the front lawn, Mr. Englewood's riding lawn mower rolled over green grass. Today he was mowing the lawn vertically. Toward the orphanage and then back toward Lake Arctic. *If only he saw what was happening, surely he'd come to the rescue*, Cal thought. But he'd just turned and was heading toward the water, his back to Cal, Hector, and the rest of the orphans.

"Hurry up," said Hector, his chest bumping the back of Cal's head. "I ain't goin' to waste all day on you. You're not the only one around here who needs to learn about rules." The crowd of orphans that had been inching closer gasped and took a step back. Hector shoved Cal headfirst out the door. Cal's arms flailed like the damaged wings of a bird attempting unsuccessfully to take flight as he fell down the concrete front steps.

Cal scuffed his knee on the bottom step.

Sitting up, he faced Hector, who smirked down at him from the top step. Any second he'd pounce and put his fists to work. Cal looked down, away from Hector, and saw blood from his knee trickling down his leg, sweat smearing the blood on his shin. Seeing his own blood woke him up.

Cal scrambled to his feet, acting on instincts now, and dashed across the front lawn to Aunt Robbie. Hardly slowing, he stumbled up her trunk, pulling on branches with his hands and arms until he was as high—and as far from Hector—as he could go.

"Torch, Torch, Torch. You think stupid old Roberta's gonna protect you? You gotta come down sometime." Hector stomped over to the maple tree so he could look up and watch Cal from the grass below. Cal could see Hector, too, and he was still smirking. He rubbed his right fist into the palm of his left hand.

Cal watched him from thirty feet above, not knowing what to do. He turned and peered through the leaves at Mr. Englewood, riding away into the sun and the black, orange-cracked Mantle.

"Hey! Up there! What're you looking at? You got bigger bones to fry than the loony lawn mower."

Through the leaves Cal could just make out some of

the other orphans, spilling out the front door now, straining their necks to see, squinting as they tried to spot red hair amidst green foliage.

Fight! Fight! Fight! Fight! Fight!

Cal only wished Aunt Robbie was a taller tree. He wanted to go higher and farther away.

"Torch! You listening?" Hector shouted. "We gotta talk about rules."

Crouching like a catcher on Aunt Robbie the maple tree's highest branch, Cal didn't say anything. He watched Mr. Englewood slowly—oh so slowly—progress toward Lake Arctic, and he couldn't help but remember a scene from years ago, the morning of the day he left the outside world for Robert. He remembered the dampness of that morning, the coolness. He remembered, of course, the pink earthworm making its way across the street. He remembered, finally, how he'd felt that morning, how badly he wanted the earthworm to make it. How helpless he had felt knowing there was nothing he could do but sit and wait and watch. How, as the blue Taurus pulled up to the curb and the earthworm still hadn't made it, Cal had had so little control over what would happen next. The earthworm's fate had felt so crucial to Cal's life that morning, and yet there was nothing he could do about it.

And here he was again, with no control over his situation. A fourteen-year-old beast howled at him from below, and all he could do was sit and wait and watch Mr. Englewood on his lawn mower moving slowly away from him. Oh, if only Mr. Englewood could make it to the shore and turn back around!

"Fine, then," Hector said below. "You ain't coming down, I'm coming up." And he stepped onto Aunt Robbie's trunk. He used his hands and feet, climbing like a cougar. Under his shirt, Hector's muscular shoulder blades rolled back and forward as he climbed.

In another minute, Mr. Englewood would reach the rock beach and head back toward the school. If Cal could just survive until then.

As always, Cal knew, it was out of his control.

But wait a minute. Was it really? This time, for so many reasons, Cal wasn't so sure. He now had two friends in the world, and he had skipped a stone just that morning, hadn't he? Perhaps there was something he could do.

Perhaps it was time he took some control.

Cal's mind raced. He was about to be mauled high up in a tree, and any alternative looked promising. Nothing out there through the leaves was as scary as Hector climbing deliberately, powerfully, menacingly up the tree. Cal shifted backward, away from the ascending beast. He wobbled and remembered where he was—that he had no place to go. Taking a deep breath, he shoved his hand in his pocket and closed his fingers around his stone. The stone slid between his pointer finger and thumb. That morning, holding the stone had calmed Cal, reassured him. Now it gave him confidence. And he knew what he had to do.

Cal jumped.

He dropped through branches and the few leaves near Aunt Robbie's trunk. His heart forgot to drop with him, rising into his throat like a passenger gravity forgot in a descending elevator. As the ground rose up to him, Cal had time to second-guess his decision. He hadn't realized how high thirty feet really was.

Twenty feet from the branch he'd jumped off of, Cal met Hector, who stood up tall in fear, eyes wide. Cal's feet landed on Hector's chest and drove him backward and down, down, down.

Hector landed with a thud on his back, his body breaking Cal's fall.

"Uh," Hector groaned. He coughed, and Cal rolled away from him and got to his feet, not daring to stick around and make sure the bully was down for the count. Hector was still breathing; Cal knew that meant it was time to scram.

Cal ran.

He ran away from Hector. He ran away from the orphanage. He passed the orphans on his left. Many of whom, though stunned, were clapping for him. But Cal, he didn't acknowledge them. He just ran.

He ran faster than ever before. The pounding of his feet nearly matching the pounding of his heart.

"Torch?" Hector managed behind him. "Torch? Torch!"

Cal heard Berneatha's voice: "Whey you goin', Calvin Cobble?"

He wasn't heading for Lake Arctic.

He wasn't even heading for Mr. Englewood's shack, where no one would follow him.

He was heading where no one ever headed.

He was heading for the Shadow.

Chapter 30

As he reached it—it, the deep, absolute darkness known in Robert as the Shadow—Cal had second thoughts. He threw on the breaks, forcing his head and shoulders backward and away from the darkness. His feet slid out from underneath him and swung up above his eye line, and he was airborne, arms flailing. He landed on his shoulder blades first, his head snapped back into the ground, and then his lower body crashed, too. Instantly, coldness seeped into his toes and up to his ankles.

Cal sat up on his elbows and looked down.

He didn't have any feet.

He examined his body, from green T-shirt and blue denim short-pants all the way down to his bare legs. But there were no dirty tennis shoes to be seen. The Shadow had amputated them.

Cal remembered Belinda Poof—how she'd stepped

into the Shadow and vanished forever. Right then, all Cal wanted was his feet back. Looking down and not seeing them, though, he somehow forgot how to move his legs.

Swallowing back fear, Cal grabbed underneath his knee with both hands and yanked. There it was—his foot—the dirty tennis shoe—still intact. He wiggled his toes. Everything still worked.

Cal repeated the process with his left leg. The toes wiggled. Everything worked.

Cal heard noises behind him. Groaning and yelling. It had to be Hector. Cal didn't want to look back. That's when he made up his mind. The Shadow hadn't taken his feet from him, and maybe he could survive in there for a while—twenty minutes, an hour at the most—while Hector and everyone else went to class. It would give him some time to come up with a plan.

Yes. It was the only way.

Cal stood up. He poked his finger into the Shadow, watched it disappear. He pulled it back, and he still had the finger. The noises got louder behind him, and he knew he didn't have much time.

Cal closed his eyes and took two long steps.

* * *

Cold and nothing.

Cold is how he felt—thoroughly, unavoidably cold. Nothing is what he saw when he opened his eyes.

Standing still, afraid to move, Cal shivered in the densest shadow in the world as he tried to make out figures of trees or anything else. Nothing. The darkness was absolute.

It is important to distinguish absolute darkness from the very, very dark. There are many very, very dark places. If you get up in the middle of some sleepless night when your house has visited the Land of Nod, Sleep's deep breaths the only sounds anywhere in the abode, it may seem absolutely dark. It's not. The street light is on or maybe the lawn light. Such light penetrates door cracks and curtained windows. Digital clocks gleam green. The darkness is not absolute.

In the Shadow, on the left side of Earth's pit, the darkness is absolute.

Cal lifted his hand and touched his nose with his palm. He could feel his damp skin and, when his palm brushed his lips, taste his salty sweat, but he couldn't see his fingers even as they brushed his eyelashes.

He shivered again, and not just from the cold. He knew, rationally, that if he turned around and walked straight ahead, he'd be back in the sunlight. But he couldn't go back—not with his life as an orphan back there. Not with Hector back there. And the absolute darkness was beginning to disorient him. A sick fear took over, signaled by a clammier sweat than that brought on by his dash across the lawn. As the sweats mixed and ran cold on his skin in the 67-degree cool of the Shadow, Cal wondered if in a few minutes he would still be able to turn around and find the lighted world.

He thought right then of Belinda Poof, and he felt

it was worth a shot: "Belinda," Cal whisper-shouted. "Belinda Poof?"

Of course, nothing. He was alone. As alone as a boy can be in or on this world.

The weight of it all, the ramifications of the decision he needed to make in the next few moments—to go deeper into the nothingness and never return, as Belinda must have inadvertently chosen, or return to the light for what would surely be a bloodier death at the hands of the school bully, whom he'd kicked to the ground but who would surely recover—brought Cal to his knees, to cold hard dirt, where all he could do was bury his face in the hands he couldn't see.

He squeezed his hand into his jeans pocket and grabbed his stone, flat and just short of a full circle. And then—oh most blessed and then! (a storyteller's favorite words)—and then he heard a voice.

Chapter 31

Here's how it looked from the point of view of any Hidden Shores orphan not named Cobble, Twiggins, or Nelson.

When the kid with the flaming hair stepped into—no, he didn't, did he?—the Shadow, nobody said a thing. Gulps and gasps replaced words and even screams for help. The little braniac with the pigtails stomped toward the Shadow a few steps and stopped. She yelled the lost boy's name. Then she pivoted and raced over to Hector, who was still on the ground, and kicked him over and over, in the ribs and the head. Man, that girl's got big feet. All he could do was groan and protect his face with his arms. "Now look what you've done!" she yelled. "He's gone, you big brute, gone!" She kept on kicking.

She wouldn't have stopped, either, if Mr. Bruno, from behind us, hadn't said, "Little missus, mind yourself. That ain't the way."

He eased down the front steps, pulled Twiggins away from Hector, and walked—no, he jogged; Mr. Bruno jogged!—across the lawn to the Shadow, faster than he did when Belinda Poof disappeared. He hollered, "Kid! Kid! Get back here! I ain't losing another one!"

When nobody answered, Mr. Bruno dropped his head and muttered to himself for what felt like an eternity.

Then he went crazy.

He turned and skipped toward Lake Arctic, looking toward the Shadow and yelling, "You get on back here. You got to hear me! Come on now, kid. I ain't gonna lose you," and such things until he was almost to the water— right by Mr. E's shack! He crouched down there, rolled a smoke, and blew two streams through his nostrils. I guess that was his way of saying good-bye. He studied the grass all the way back to the orphanage.

Sayonara, Cobble.

Chapter 32

Kid! Kid! Get back here. I ain't losing another one."
It sounded like—Mr. Bruno?

"Uh, I'm—I'm here," Cal said. After a long moment, he added, "I can't come back, though. At least here, Hector won't come after me."

When Mr. Bruno spoke again, his voice was softer. He really was close. "Now you listen to me. I know a place you can go till you figure things out. You just need to follow my voice till we get there, okay? I'll hoop and holler and won't nobody think to follow. Got it?"

And that's how it went.

Cal walked through the chilly darkness, his arms in front of him, hands feeling for obstacles, following Mr. Bruno's shouts: "You get on back here," he yelled. Then, "You got to hear me!" and "Come on now, kid. I ain't gonna lose you."

It went this way for several minutes, Cal cautiously

moving forward as he followed the phys ed instructor's voice, and then Mr. Bruno's voice was soft again: "Okay. We're here. All you need to do now is wait. In fifteen minutes, I'll have all your pardners back inside. That's when you make a break for it. Don't take too long blinking your vision back. Don't want anyone to see you, now, hear?"

Cal watched twin streams of cigarette smoke drift toward him and dissolve.

Chapter 33

Twelve Years Ago

It was a long fall, some three hundred feet. As he fell, Jeffrey knew full well he may have been living the last few seconds of his life. He was surprisingly okay with knowing this. What he wasn't okay with was risking his brother's life. But it didn't seem like he'd had a choice. Herschel wouldn't have made it much longer up in the thin air on top of the screw.

It is often said that a person's life flashes before his eyes right before he dies. That time slows down and the person whose life is about to end sees a big-screen movie of all the important people and events from his life.

Jeffrey wasn't remembering anything as he fell.

All he was thinking about was saving his brother and about the ridge of the golden screw, rushing up to meet them.

Ta-thunk.

Jeffrey's feet hit first, and then he fell on his backside.

Miraculously, Jeffrey's bulky lime-green jacket absorbed most of the fall's impact. Jeffrey held Herschel to his chest, and they began sliding. This was, incredibly, how Jeffrey had hoped it would work out moments before, running to the edge of the groove with Herschel in his arms. He'd remembered then the third of Bartholomew Rogers' Three Important (and Simple!) Things to Remember for Antarctic Survival:

Stuff your jacket or snowsuit with marshmallows.
Marshmallow is the best insulator around.

Jeffrey had hoped the marshmallows he'd stuffed into his lime-green jacket two weeks before were as good at breaking falls as they were at keeping people warm. Until he'd jumped, he hadn't had time to consider what would happen if marshmallow wasn't good at breaking falls.

They had landed on the ridge of the screw, and now they were spiraling down it. A screw's ridge wraps around and around the screw from the base of its head all the way to its bottom tip. For Jeffrey and Herschel, the ridge had become a golden playground slide from above the clouds to the snowy ground of the South Pole.

Jeffrey patted his brother on the chest. "Come on, Herschel. Wake up, now," he said. "Everything's gonna be okay."

They slid down and around the screw. They accelerated with each revolution, the air getting thicker as they descended.

Jeffrey could taste the difference. He'd become so accustomed to the thin air above the clouds that breathing the dense air below them was refreshing, like drinking water.

Herschel came to. His first breaths came with difficulty and sounded like snores. His lungs were fighting hard for each one. Finally, he spoke. "Jeff. Jeff," he said. "What's happening?"

"What's happening, Herschel? You about to be the first one to see what's underneath this screw."

"What? Where are we?" And then Herschel looked around and realized, though he didn't quite believe.

Down and around they went, faster and faster. The cold air slapped their faces, but now they didn't mind. Even Antarctic wind couldn't spoil their fun.

"Pretty cool, huh, kid brother?" Jeffrey asked.

"Yeah—not so scary once you get the hang of it," Herschel said, sitting up now. "Wee!" he chirped.

"Yeehaw!" Jeffrey shrieked.

It was exhilarating to slide down the winding ridge. The brothers giggled as they descended down and around the golden screw, faster than any Olympic bobsled team.

Jeffrey held Herschel to his chest, keeping him safe.

Chapter 34

Help made it to Bart's Screw. The day before he arrived in Antarctica, the President had ordered all major American airlines to cancel their flights and dispatch their planes to the South Pole. The people in the groove—who had unscrewed a screw so long it had broken right through the clouds and kept going—were dropped off near the boats they'd arrived on, which then carried them home. Nobody cared that they didn't get to see what was underneath the screw. If asked months later if they had any regrets, nearly every one of them would have expressed gratitude and pride for the opportunity to support such a global cause and then relief to be alive and back home, keeping up with further developments in Antarctica on TV.

After dropping passengers off near their boats, pilots took their planes back up to the head of the screw. They released long ropes and circled the screw, so that their ropes got tangled into knots all around it. Then the planes tipped their noses up and headed for the stars.

Bart's Screw lifted with them. The pilots took their planes up, up, and away from the deep hole in the middle of Antarctica. From above the clouds, as high as the planes could safely fly, flight attendants on each plane cut their ropes loose, and the screw fell. The bottom tip hit the snow first, and then the massive thing fell on its side. A cloud of snow mist wafted up all the way to the planes, enveloping them for several minutes, blinding the pilots, who prayed they didn't crash into each other.

When the mist cleared, they still couldn't see the great golden screw in its entirety. It was too big. It stretched across all of Antarctica and still farther. The head and tip ran off opposite ends of the continent, over the ocean.

Chapter 35

After narrowly escaping two more car accidents, Ron Cobble finally settled in Second Sun Bank's parking lot. At least his car had settled. He was a nervous wreck, having almost collided with four cars in three minutes. Car horns squawked in his ears. His vision was blurry. He'd sweated through the back of his shirt and jacket, and he was sticking to the driver seat. He took a deep breath, opened his car door, extended his left foot to the pavement, and peeled himself from his car seat.

HONK!

A big loud yellow truck screamed into the parking spot next to Ron's, squealing to a halt in front of Ron's door. The truck pulsed like a living thing. Its engine grunted impatiently. Ron closed his door to let the truck in. He got out once it was parked and waved his apology to the driver. The driver of the big loud yellow truck glared at him. For a moment, Ron thought he recognized the man. He didn't know from where.

There were five tellers working the front desk and five lines of people in front of the tellers. Each line had two or three people in it, and Ron picked the closest one. The driver of the truck that had almost taken off Ron's door got in the next line. Ron was immediately intimidated. The man was young and thick with muscles. His arms were about as big as Ron's legs, and his neck was connected to his shoulders by protruding muscles. But it was the man's massive, flaccid face that was most memorable. His forehead was large and flat, pushed out from the rest of his face like the brow of a Neanderthal Ron remembered seeing fifteen years earlier in a high school history textbook. The man's eyes were small and green, like peas pushed into the middle of his doughy face. His cheeks sagged below his jaw line like a bulldog's. Had Ron seen him before?

Ron extended his hand to the man. "I'm . . . you know . . . Sally," he said. "I—I mean I'm soggy. I mean I'm sorry."

The man rolled his pea-eyes and turned away from Ron. He stuffed his hands into the pockets of his black denim jacket, denying Ron a handshake. The right pocket bulged, and Ron wondered what, besides the man's hand, was in it. The man muttered something about "Sally."

He must be having a bad day, Ron thought. He knew what that was like. He wasn't having the greatest day himself.

"Next," the teller in front of Ron announced. She

looked to be in her teens, probably just out of high school. Ron walked, unprepared, to the front desk. In order to withdraw cash, he needed to know his account number at the bank. He never remembered the number, but he had it written down on a scrap of paper that he kept buried in one of his pants pockets.

"Good morning," he said. "Cash." He dug into his right front pocket for the slip of paper. There were several slips of paper in the pocket—including a grocery receipt, post-it notes from work, and his and Julia's fortune-cookie fortunes from the previous evening (they'd shared Chinese takeout)—and Ron wasn't sure which one the account number was written on. He stretched his neck, trying to see into the pocket.

"What is this?" the teller's voice shrieked.

"Hold up," Ron said, looking back up at her.

Oh, if only, for once in his life, Ron had said what he meant—"hold on," in this case.

"Security!" she yelled.

And then a gunshot pierced the air.

Ron, of course, hadn't pulled the trigger. He didn't even own a gun. He was withdrawing cash so he and his wife could go to dinner. He was not attempting to rob the bank.

But the man in the line next to Ron was attempting to rob the bank. The same man who'd almost taken off the door of Ron's car minutes earlier. The man with the sagging, bulldog cheeks.

And while Ron was looking down into his pocket,

the young teller in front of him had seen the man with the bulldog cheeks pull a gun out of his pocket and point it at another teller. She'd assumed Ron was about to do the same thing. After she yelled for security, the bulldog-man with the gun took a shot at her.

Luckily, he'd missed. She'd ducked under the counter before she'd even finished her scream.

Someone grabbed Ron from behind and slapped handcuffs around his wrists.

"What—what's happening?" Ron sputtered. "I—"

"You have the right to remain silent," a gruff voice cut him off. "And I recommend you do."

* * *

Later, the security guards proudly reported to anyone who'd listen that they'd apprehended Mutt McGee, the notorious bank robber and murderer, and his until-now-unknown accomplice: Ron Cobble.

Mad Mutt's picture had been in the local paper seven times in the last two months for other more successful bank robberies. In the process of robbing those banks, he'd shot and killed three tellers and two security guards. The worst day of Ron Cobble's life (up to then, anyway) would go down in the record books as a happy day for the rest of the country. One of America's most feared bad guys had finally been brought to justice. This to go with the unscrewing of Bart's Screw that very hour. Yes, a happy day.

"To our knowledge, this Cobble guy is Mad Mutt's

only partner," a policeman reported.

"He told me it was a hold up, and I just yelled for help," the young teller-turned-heroine told the press.

Chapter 36

This Very Year
(Twelve Years After Unscrewing Bart's Screw)

After waiting for what seemed hours upon hours, Cal took a step forward. The light hit him like a bomb in his brain, shrieking and excruciating. His eyes squeezed shut of their own volition, and he wondered if they'd ever open again. And then he was up in the air in somebody's long, strong arms. It didn't take long for Cal to figure out who those long, strong arms belonged to.

"Mr. Englewood?"

"You just keep them eyes shut tighter than Tupperware, Cal. You be all right."

* * *

"You can open them eyes now, Cal. Take your time."

Cal first opened his eyes to a squint. When they adjusted to the gray of Mr. Englewood's shack, he opened them all the way. And there he was. After nearly half an hour in the scariest place in Robert—yes, in the world—he now found himself in the second scariest: Mr. E's shack, down by the water. Except Cal wasn't scared. At that moment, in fact, there was no place inside the world he would rather have been.

It was as small as it looked from the outside. A single hammock, on which Cal now sat and swayed, occupied the middle of the shack, its ends nailed to diagonal corners of the room. The wood floor was dark, its wax peeling. The residence's one window, rectangular, faced Lake Arctic. Mr. Englewood had taped newspaper over it, presumably to ease Cal's transition back to sight. The newspaper was yellow and crinkled, and, Cal now realized, it wasn't the only newspaper in the room.

Stacks of old newspapers lined the walls of the shack, leaving hardly enough room next to the door for a toaster oven and, on top of it, a kerosene stove and stainless steel griddle. The cooking appliances sat atop cans of soup, chili, corn, and mixed vegetables. Half a loaf of white bread, a jar of peanut butter, and a gallon jug of distilled water nestled against the cans.

"Enough to make a man reconsider a career in lawn mowing, isn't it?"

"You mean that food," Cal said, "that's what the orphanage pays you?"

"That and a place to live, Cal Cobble, and it's not your orphanage who pays me. No sir. I'm employed by the city of Robert."

"But—but I don't get it, Mr. Englewood. I mean,

well, no offense, really, but, I mean, why would anyone want to live here?"

Mr. Englewood's eyes found the door and stayed on it for awhile. When they returned to Cal's eyes, Mr. Englewood said, "You right. It don't make a whole lot of sense. But I got my reasons for being here, same's you. Ironic thing is, I know why the both of us is here—knew who you were the moment you told me your name, Cobble— and you don't even know your own reasons, not fully.

"But we'll get to that later. Based on that scene you and Walter made out there today, I got the feeling you're staying around for some time—am I right?"

"I mean, if it's okay—"

"Then I suppose it's time you learned some things. No use sitting around doing nothing. I assume you wanna try your hand at skipping another stone tomorrow?"

Cal nodded.

"Tomorrow morning, we skip stones. Then you read a newspaper."

Chapter 37

Twelve Years Ago

What was found underneath Bart's Screw wasn't, initially, very exciting. It looked just about like nothing. The deep, funneling hole seemed just that—a hole. The bottom of the hole seemed to be just rock. And not even precious rock, like diamond or ruby or even amethyst. No one was sure, at first, what kind of rock it was.

It took a full day of extensive testing before the planet's best geologists figured out the bottom of the hole was made of feldspar, which is what the moon is made of. And it took another week before anyone understood what it was they'd found.

Chapter 38

"What do you mean it's the core?" the President said into the phone, talking to his head geologist.

"We think it's Earth's core, sir," the geologist repeated.

"Are you sure? I thought the core was made of some kind of metal."

"Yes, sir—mostly iron and nickel—that's been the hypothesis. But we're pretty sure this here is it."

"What's it doing down there? I mean isn't it supposed to be in the middle of the planet somewhere?"

"Yes sir, it is—and we think it was. We think it used to sit on the tip of Bart's Screw." The geologist paused before continuing. "Sir, we also think it was probably stuck between the two screws—Bart's and Santa's, I mean—kind of like a globe."

"Well," the President said, curious that he was beginning to accept what the geologist was telling him, "let's find out for sure."

The President didn't know what to think. It all sounded pretty far-fetched. But if this incredible new concept of Earth science turned out to be accurate, he had an incredible vision to match.

Chapter 39

This Very Year
(Twelve Years After Unscrewing Bart's Screw)

The next morning, Cal found three stones he liked and got two of them to skip. Mr. Englewood skipped his five stones across Lake Arctic, and they called it a morning.

Upon returning to Mr. Englewood's shack, the owner of the house loped to the far left corner of the room, tilted a stack of newspapers, and yanked the bottom one free. He handed the brittle pages to Cal: "What do you know about how this place came to be?"

"You—you mean your house?"

"That's a short story, and it's about as interesting as cloud watching in Robert. No, I don't mean this falling-apart shack. I mean all of it. What do you know about how all of this came to be—your orphanage and this city?"

Cal, like the other Hidden Shores orphans, didn't know anything about the history of Robert. Principal

Warden insisted that there was no use looking behind them. As orphans, he said, they didn't have a past. They were better off looking ahead. Maybe, just maybe, they'd have a future. The day the blue Taurus with the foggy interior and the seat belt that smelled like armpit picked him up at the curb in front of the Detroit orphanage, Cal had known only that he was headed to some other orphanage. Imagine his surprise, Cal asked Mr. Englewood, when he boarded a plane and then a helicopter and, after a full day of travel, found himself dropping to the pit of the earth. Each Hidden Shores orphan, as far as he knew, shared a similar story. They lived where they lived, and after awhile they got used to it and stopped asking questions.

Mr. Englewood listened carefully, waiting for Cal to finish before he responded. "It's time you did some catching up, Cal Cobble. Each of these newspapers hit the presses twelve years ago. That means I have just about every day from the last part of that year chronicled here."

From Mr. Englewood's twelve-year-old newspaper, Cal learned for the very first time about bearded explorer Bartholomew Rogers and his odd discovery. He read everything else in that paper, too. "Cover to cover, Cal. You need some context," Mr. Englewood said. Cal read about the Tar Heels' national championship in basketball, about the heat wave that had swallowed America's east coast, about the newest thriller in the local Cineplex, about how to make sugar-free ice cream—in a coffee can!— that the whole family would love, about the partisan wars in the US Senate, and finally he landed on a particularly harrowing story about a hideously violent bank robbery and the perpetrator on the lam. There was a picture of the doughy, jowly-faced villain next to the column, and underneath the picture the name McGee.

"Mr. Englewood," Cal asked, looking up from the newspaper, "whatever happened to Bartholomew Rogers, the explorer? He's mentioned here a bunch of times."

"It's a good question, Cal. One I can't answer. You hear him grumble a few times over the next maybe twenty papers. He always sour—doesn't want to talk to anyone. Then he just disappears."

Cal nodded and dropped his eyes again to the newspaper. He read lying on his back on Mr. Englewood's cot. Mr. Englewood had stepped outside to mow the lawn, and the drone of the riding lawn mower was constant in the background. When he'd read every word in the issue, he dropped it on his chest, crossed his hands under the back of his head, and thought about it all, feeling satisfied that he'd completed a task that day. Mr. Englewood had advised Cal to read one paper a day. In three months, he'd not only know a whole lot more about Robert, Mr. Englewood told him—not to mention himself—he'd understand what he knew. "You got to let it all sink in, Cal. Give a tomato seed three months' water in one day, you drown it. Give it its daily allotment, and in a couple months you have something to savor. You have tomato juice and tomato soup and chili and marinara sauce and tomato slices for your sandwiches. Real knowledge you can use all over the place."

For three months, Cal's days with Mr. Englewood looked like this:

Cal woke up to Mr. Englewood's laughter. Cal slept under Mr. Englewood's cot—the only space in the room big enough for sleeping—and used his shoes for a pillow. Shoes make a pretty comfortable pillow, if you rest your head on the top of them and not the bottom. They also leave deep marks on your face that take fifteen minutes to fade. According to Mr. Englewood, Cal woke up every morning looking "like somebody thought you was a soccer ball."

As Mr. Englewood laughed, he and Cal stepped out the front door to the Robertian morning—a black, orange-cracked sky and a ray of sunlight from the shore of Lake Arctic to as far out as they could see. Cal asked, every morning, if today was the day he skipped his stone. Mr. Englewood, every morning, said no. The first few mornings, Mr. Englewood spoke to Cal while they skipped; he taught and reassured him. But quickly they developed silent rhythms, each knowing what the other was trying to accomplish. Cal got to see Mr. Englewood skip his stones clear across the great lake; Mr. Englewood got to see Cal improve. On the seventh day, Cal skipped a stone nine times. On the forty-third day, he skipped one nineteen times. How thrilling it was for Cal to watch his own stone bound across the flat water; to hear the pleasing percussive shushing sound each time it touched down; to admire the way it stood up and skied, veering to the right, before finally dropping beneath the water's surface.

Before the wake-up bell clanged at Hidden Shores and people might spot the two of them through a window, they hid themselves between Mr. Englewood's shack and the water. There they filled the lawn mower with gas and moved systematically through the necessary checkups and repairs.

When the lawn mower was ready to go, Cal squeezed through Mr. Englewood's lone window, tugged the appropriate newspaper free from the middle of a tall pile—he was reading them chronologically—and spent the day learning about the outside world, from the perspective of eastern North Carolina, in the months leading up to America's awarding Alaska the city of Robert. Often, Cal rolled his stone over his fingers as he read. When he finished the paper, he dropped it on his chest, crossed his hands behind his head, thought about what he'd read, and waited for Mr. Englewood to finish mowing the lawn.

After two months, Cal began noticing something different in the newspapers he read each day. In each day's paper, in the National News section, articles were missing; they had been cut out completely. After three days of noticing missing articles, Cal brought the subject up to Mr. Englewood.

"Mr. Englewood," Cal asked when his friend came in from lawn-mowing to get a drink of water. "How come there's no article here?" He pointed to the rect-angular hole in the page. "Or here? I mean, there were articles cut out of yesterday's paper, too. And the day before's."

"Yes, Cal," said Mr. Englewood, his eyes dropping to the floor. "You're right. That first night you got here, to my shack? I went in and cut out articles about one par-ticular story. Can't stand censorship, but I'm just not sure you're ready to hear this story yet. You will be, though. Just trust me and give it some time, huh?"

Cal nodded. He wasn't sure what to say. He knew his friend was looking out for him, and he decided to ignore the missing articles as best he could.

For dinner every evening, Mr. Englewood made a can of soup or chili—into which they dipped toasted bread—and can of vegetables. They drank straight from the bottle of distilled water. As they ate, Cal asked questions, and Mr. Englewood did his best to fill in the blanks in Cal's understanding. "You'll learn most of this as you read, but I don't suppose you can wait now, can you? Where, you ask, are those screws? They're back where they started, top and bottom of the globe, only the screw tails were melted down and removed, and the top one—Santa's, as they say—they painted it black underneath, so we can't see it from down here. 'An eyesore,' they said. Can you imagine? We look up and all we see all day is black rock and some oozing orange lava, and they think a little gold in the heavens gonna put us off?"

After dinner, when the orphans were asleep, Cal and Mr. Englewood bathed in warm Lake Arctic with a bottle of biodegradable shampoo that went under the cot when Cal wasn't sleeping there.

And then they woke up and did it all over again.

Chapter 40

Three months passed methodically yet hastily. There was method: One newspaper a day, another skip or two nearly every morning. And yet the months became a blur. They were the best three months of Cal's life, and they raced by him as if he were walking on the side of the freeway, each day a speeding car. At the end of these three months, Cal knew as much as the *Carolina Courier* could tell him about how Robert came to be. Curiosity in its truest form, however, is never satisfied, and Cal still had questions:

"So it was the President's idea to put us down here?"

"Not us, Cal. Not you and not me. His idea was to put criminals, the most dangerous ones in America, at the Pit of the Planet, where they couldn't inflict more harm on the country's decent citizens. Robert Inner-planet Penitentiary—R-I-P!—that was his idea. Hard to disagree with that, huh? No, the President's a good man, Cal."

"Okay. Then why are we here?"

"You're here because you need a place to live. Am I right? Your Principal Warden, he saw an opportunity for a school and proposed that America use the space right. Criminals kept in the dark, America's youth in the light. That's about as pretty a metaphor as you're gonna find, wouldn't you say? Problem is, when it came time to tell the country about this new school—Hidden Shores—nobody wanted to be the one who told. I mean, pretty as the metaphor is, the more lawmakers thought about it, Americans don't want to hear there's a bunch of kids sharing an island with dangerous criminals. And good people, they certainly don't want to think about dangerous criminals, anyway—that's why the criminals were dropped down here in the first place. So lawmakers never told anyone about this place—about what's here at the center of the Earth. They stopped talking about it altogether. You know, even if people did want to visit you all, see it for themselves, they couldn't do it. Nobody's allowed here, not even to enforce those academic standards other schools beholden to. You probably get the sense your school's not up to snuff, as they say, huh? It's not that bad, though, Cal. You be out of here by the time you turn fifteen. Off to some boarding school."

"Yeah, I know. That's just—it's just a long way out there, you know? And you're not gonna let me stay here with you for two and a half years, are you?" Cal paused, looked down at his sneakers. "I—I still don't know why you're here, Mr. Englewood."

"You don't need me to tell you. It's in the next paper—the most recent one. Ain't that a thing? Twelve-year-old rag, newest one I got. You wanna take a deep breath before you read that one, Cal. You'll learn something about me—and you'll learn something about yourself, too."

He picked the final paper off the top of a stack and handed it to Cal.

Cal leafed through it and saw that no articles had been cut out of this one.

"It's got a couple names you'll know. I circled the headlines, see? You'll read about a guy named Cobble. And you'll read about my brother, Jeffrey Englewood, the bravest man I ever knew."

Chapter 41

Twelve Years Ago

The defendant will burst through the courtroom doors any moment now," said the CourtroomTV broadcaster in a hushed voice. "He and his partner, Mr. Mad Mutt McGee, will be tried separately. Too dangerous to put them in a room full of people together."

"And there he is now," she said, her voice barely audible. "You've seen his face on the news and in your papers, of course. That full head of thick red hair. Those menacing green eyes. He's shaking now, his handcuffs jangling, but don't be fooled. Don't waste your time with remorse. This is a bad man responsible for much heartbreak. Remember the money he stole, the lives he ended."

Someone not connected to the case may have found the broadcaster's whispers amusing; she was, after all, reporting not from the courtroom but from a television studio. The broadcaster, like all other viewers, was watching the proceedings on TV.

Julia Cobble, however, didn't pay attention to the broadcaster. She was very much connected to the case. Her husband had this one chance to clear his name and return to her, and he had never responded well under pressure. He just could never come up with the right words. Lying on her back in her hospital room, she watched Ron twitch, his eyes on the ground. She knew he was trying to collect himself.

Julia herself struggled to focus. Complications in her pregnancy had forced the hospital to hold her the rest of the way. Once the Cobbles' son was born—Calvin, they'd decided to call him—and both mother and son were deemed healthy, they could go home. Julia was sick all the time these days and constantly dizzy. She forced her eyes to stay on the small, round-shouldered man she loved—the man up there on the television who had been charged with several murders as Mad Mutt McGee's accomplice.

He sat down next to the defense attorney at a table facing the judge. No sooner had he sat than the judge asked all in the room to rise.

"I've received a note here—let me see," said the CourtroomTV broadcaster. "Apparently, the judge has requested to speak directly to Mr. Cobble and not his attorney just yet."

The judge cleared his throat, looked directly at Ron, and said, "Given the particularly gruesome and public nature of these charges, Mr. Cobble, I'd like to hear from you first. What, sir, is your plea?"

"Oh no," Julia said. "Don't make him try to find the word."

Ron Cobble looked up, his hands still shaking in their handcuffs.

"Innocent!" Julia yelled at the TV. "You're innocent!"

But when Ron spoke, that's not what he said. "Guilty"—that's what he said. Flashbulbs flickered around the courtroom as reporters gasped.

"He admits it!"

"He doesn't even want to defend himself!"

"What a monster!"

"A wicked, wicked man!"

"So that's it, then," the broadcaster said, her voice louder now. "All that needs to be figured out now is Mr. Cobble's sentence."

Before tears flooded her eyes, Julia read her husband's lips, his words blocked out by the commotion in the courtroom.

"I mean innocent," he mouthed.

Chapter 42

The President's helicopter alighted on the snow and ice that had, a day before, been buried under the head of the screw. With a triumphant smile spread across his face, the President stumbled out and walked toward the crater-like hole where the screw had been.

There, looking over the edge of the hole, was a boy dressed in lime-green frosted with white snow. The President said, "Hello?" and then, to himself, "Where did you come from, young man?" When he got closer, he heard the boy's whimpering.

The President put a hand on the whimpering boy's shoulder and asked, "Are you all right, son?" The boy didn't respond right away, so the President patted the boy's shoulder. He shook the boy gently.

The boy looked up. Tears were frozen to his face, and his eyes were watery.

He looked like his heart had been shattered. It

appeared, in that instant, that no amount of love, comfort, or support could glue the boy's heart back together.

The boy said, "Jeff was right. I was the first to see it."

Chapter 43

This Very Year
(Twelve Years After Unscrewing Bart's Screw)

"So this guy, Ron, he has the same last name as me," Cal said.

"Uh-huh."

"And he's a bank robber."

"That's what the article says, I'm afraid. You read it same as me."

"But—Mr. Englewood?" Cal looked down at the newspaper, at the mug shot of Ron Cobble. "He's—he's my dad. I mean I don't know, uh, anything about my parents, but I know their names. They gave me those when I was out there at the other orphanage. My dad's name is Ronald, the same as the bank robber's name. And it says here he, well, he has a wife, Julia. That's my mom's name."

"Yeah. I had a feeling that might be the case, Cal. First time I saw you, I saw your daddy's eyes. Heck, I been staring at these newspapers for so long, I remember just about every word and face. And then you said your last name, and you being an orphan, I guess a lot of pieces fit." Mr. Englewood grabbed from a pile of newspapers the Swiss Army knife he used to open his cans of food. This time, he peeled the scissors up and cut out the article about Ron Cobble and Mad Mutt McGee. "You keep this, Cal. He's your father. You decide what to do with what you learned."

Cal pocketed the article and then took a moment, letting it all settle in. His dad, a bank robber? It didn't feel right—and did that mean he was still alive?—and yet he'd never known his dad. Not for one breath of his life. He didn't know what he was supposed to feel now. A part of him felt surprisingly relieved. He'd been vaguely mad at his dad a long time, mad that his dad hadn't come for him. If he was in jail, well, that was why he'd never come for Cal, right? The more Cal thought about it, the less he knew. He knew that no matter how badly he wanted to understand it all now, he still wouldn't. And besides, there was more he needed to ask Mr. Englewood. He'd read another article, after all. "And Jeffrey Englewood," Cal said, "the only one who died in Antarctica that day—"

"My brother."

"He was your . . . I—I'm sorry, Mr. Englewood." Cal knew he should say something else. Cal's dad was in jail, sure, but it wasn't like Cal had lost him. You can't lose what you've never had. But Mr. Englewood? He'd lost his brother when he was younger than Cal. They must have been close, too, friends or whatever, if they'd traveled to the bottom of the world together. "But think of how brave he was. I mean, he must have really wanted to see that screw if he went to Antarctica."

"That's the thing, Cal. That's just it." Mr. Englewood turned and looked out the window. A hint of sunlight still came from the hole in northeastern Alaska, enough that the scene outside Mr. Englewood's shack—the lake and the dark backdrop—looked like a black-and-white photograph, the objects in the picture dark but the air around them holding light. "It wasn't his dream. It was mine. I dragged him down there, coldest spot on the planet, all the way down there for something I wanted. It was even me got that screw going, strange as it sounds. Gave it a kick, got it twisting up to the clouds. Then Jeff, he saves my life. Gives his own to do it." Mr. Englewood didn't say anything more for a full minute. He stared out the window, his figure dissolving into the darkness.

"We went spiraling around that Bartholomew Rogers' screw. I had asthma. Was wheezing to death. So Jeff took action. He jumps off the head of the screw, me in his arms. Our jackets cushioned our landing on the screw's ridge; we somehow were still alive. Honestly, I'm just reciting facts. Witnesses saw this. I was blacked out, not having breathed properly in some time. Soon's we landed on the ridge, down we went. Around, around, around. We built speed and built speed and then—the slide got to end sometime. When it did, Jeff was under me. He broke my fall. The ground, the underbelly of this bobber, the one we on top of now, broke his."

Cal couldn't follow all of what Mr. Englewood was telling him. But he understood that he'd lost his brother. That he'd watched his brother die.

"But then, Mr. Englewood, why do you live here? Doesn't it remind you of your brother every day? I mean, you can leave, right?"

"When I got old enough, Cal—that was four years later and I was sixteen—I went to the President, well, former President by then. He'd kept in touch. Checked in on me those years. I asked him how I could get here—get to Robert. Those who knew of our Bob weren't talking about it anymore, of course. No use telling kids as they dig their holes in the backyard to China that before they get there, they liable to come across a prison full of America's nastiest, most dangerous men and women. So bringing Robert up like that to the President, it wasn't the comfiest of conversations. We both felt compelled to speak in soft voices—whispers, as I remember it. But I told the President I owed it to Jeff to see this place. My big brother, he died so I could see it. I said I had no place out there, in the outside world, anyway. Didn't deserve to walk that ground, the ground my brother should still be walking on, if I hadn't pushed him to the South Pole. That's when the President told me about your school, Cal. Said it would open that fall. They could use a man to work the grounds, he said. You know, a temporary thing. Give it a try. See how I liked it." It was the first time Mr. Englewood had laughed in what seemed a very long time. It wasn't the hearty chuckle Cal now knew well, it was an amused sound more than anything, but it was something. "Been here ever since. My choice, Cal. Nobody makes me stay."

In that moment, Cal understood. "So you're with your brother here, Mr. Englewood."

Herschel Englewood turned and smiled weakly. "And you, Cal, you down here with your dad."

Chapter 44

Take a look at that date," Mr. Englewood said. He illumined the text with a flashlight. "Every dangerous American criminal from that date and on for the next eighteen months, they all were sent down here. The worst criminals, the ones you allow a twitch and they take a life, they still get sent down here once a spot opens up. Your daddy, associated as he was with that McGee, guy who killed seven people, and those just the ones we know of, he's got to be down here."

Cal felt sorry for his dad for a moment. Cal knew how bad *down here* was at the orphanage; he couldn't imagine what *down here* was like at the prison. Then Cal remembered that his dad was a bank robber and that maybe he shouldn't feel sorry for him.

"Mr. Englewood—do you think my dad, well, do you think he killed anyone?"

"Can't say I know one way or the other, of course, but

I will say this: there's not one mention of a Ron Cobble anywhere in these newspapers, not until that last few. I've read them all more times than you've ever skipped a stone, Cal—no offense—and it's always struck me as strange, Mad Mutt's partner being spotted in only one of the robberies. Doesn't seem to make much sense, does it?"

"No, I guess not. Maybe you're right." Cal felt better, allowing himself to agree that his dad possibly wasn't a murderer.

"Tell you the truth, Cal, and this is just conjecture, mind you, but since I met you, I've started to wonder if your dad was a criminal at all. You've been telling me about your propensity for getting in trouble, right? Teachers always assuming you rousing rabble when really you just about got a halo on your head?" Mr. Englewood smiled with his eyes. "Maybe it runs in the family."

Cal thought Mr. Englewood was probably right.

No, not probably. It was more than that. In that moment, Cal knew Mr. Englewood was right. Knew it for sure. It was, he realized, the first time he could remember ever being so unequivocally sure about anything except that almost-round white skipping stone he found the second morning he met Mr. E. The feeling was powerful. More than powerful, it was empowering. And then Cal knew, for sure, something else.

"Mr. Englewood, I need to go find him."

* * *

They settled the matter the following morning. The

night before, Mr. Englewood had said they should think on it and then get a good night sleep. Of course neither had slept a wink, not after what had been revealed that evening, and certainly not with Cal's proposition hanging heavy in the air, threatening to suffocate them if Mr. Englewood hadn't cracked open the window facing Lake Arctic. The bags under their eyes and the seeping headache they shared wouldn't let them forget their sleepless night.

"First thing we need to do," Mr. Englewood told Cal after they'd skipped three stones apiece and filled the lawn mower's gas tank, "is figure out exactly where in that deep Shadow we'll find the prison. Been a long time since I saw a map."

When Cal told Mr. Englewood about the map tacked to the wall in Principal Warden's office, Mr. Englewood sighed.

"Okay then. You're really ready to do this, aren't you?"

"Yeah. I'm ready. It's my dad, you know?"

"Yeah, I know. Being honest, Cal, I'm worried about me, too. I've lived next to that half the island a heck of a long time, but I sure never dreamed I'd spend any time over there . . . so when you going to get that map?"

Cal looked out the window at Lake Artic, recognizing morning daylight, then turned back to Mr. Englewood. "Actually, right now's probably as good a time as any. Everybody will be in class, and Principal Warden will be visiting classrooms. Only problem is, well, how do I get from here to there without anyone looking out a window and spotting me?" Cal pointed at his flaming red hair. "I mean, people tend to spot me."

"They do at that, Cal. Catch you red-headed, right? That's still a good one. But hey—you could always go back there the same way you came. Through the Shadow. This time, I'll be right up next to you. Follow the lawn mower's rumble and you'll be fine."

"And I'll be in there with you." It was a girl's voice. (She said it, "I'll be in they with you.")

Chapter 45

B ernie?"
Cal's pig-tailed friend climbed through the open window before anyone had time to invite her in. When she stood up inside the shack, Mr. Englewood extended his hand, introduced himself, and they shook.

"All by myself here for years, and suddenly I've become quite the host," Mr. Englewood said.

Cal was glad to see his friend, but it was time for answers.

"Uh, what're you doing here, Bernie?"

"The question, Calvin Cobble, is what are *you* doing here?"

"I like this girl," Mr. Englewood said. "She's got spunk."

Cal knew there was no point keeping any of it to himself any more. The truth was, he could use Berneatha's confidence right then. "I'll tell you, but you go first. I mean, I'm sure mine's a longer story."

"Fine. I'll go first. I guess you're right, too—mine's not a long story. Basically, ever since you ran away, I've been trying to make sense of it all. If you weren't lost and dead in the Shadow, which I figured you probably were, and you weren't up in Aunt Robbie, there was really only one place you could be. So it's taken me a while, but last night I decided maybe you were worth it and that I might at least knock on Mr. E—Mr. Englewood's door. Then I heard you both talking. And I guess that's it."

It was Cal's turn.

He told Berneatha about the last day she'd seen him—about Mr. Bruno and ending up in Mr. Englewood's shack. Then he backtracked and explained how he'd met Mr. Englewood, how he'd been sneaking out and watching him skip stones—"I knew it, Calvin Cobble. Knew you were up to something"—and how Mr. Englewood had spotted him and taught him to skip stones, too: "I mean I'm not good like he is, but usually my rocks don't sink until they've bounced a few times." Cal told Berneatha about the newspapers he read—about the history of Robert, Bart's and Santa's Screws, and what had happened to his father. He left out only what Mr. Englewood was doing in Robert, what had happened to him and his brother. That wasn't Cal's story to tell. Finally, Cal told Berneatha about his and Mr. Englewood's plan to rescue Cal's father, Ron, and that the first step was getting that map from Principal Warden.

"Yeah—I heard that part," Berneatha Twiggins said, grateful to finally know something. "So when are we going?"

Chapter 46

You ready for this?" Cal asked his seven-year-old friend. They stood just off the water facing the darkest dark in or on the planet. Cal wanted to extend his hand and watch it disappear. But a part of him still wasn't confident he'd ever get the hand back. No, better to stay out of the Shadow as much as possible.

"I can't believe you ran in there, " Berneatha said, "and all by yourself, too."

"Yeah. I can't really believe it, either, Bernie. I guess I wasn't thinking."

Berneatha nodded.

"Okay," she said, grabbing Cal's hand. "Let's do it."

They stepped together into the Shadow, each taking two deliberate steps into 67-degree nothingness.

"All right, kids," Mr. Englewood said, turning the ignition. The engine puttered and then roared. "I'll take it slow."

And that's the way they went, Berneatha squeezing Cal's hand so hard he thought his skeleton might shriek, Mr. Englewood maintaining a steady pace and rumble as he rolled through the sunlight that was so close and yet seemed like it wasn't there at all.

"It's cold," Berneatha said.

"I know. We'll be out if it soon."

"Are we gonna run into any trees?"

"I didn't on the way down here."

"Guess trees need sunlight, just like humans do," she reasoned. "Hey—last time you were out here—you didn't see, I mean hear, Belinda did you?"

"Wish I had, Bernie."

Then Mr. Englewood's voice: "Here you are—right up next to your orphanage. I'll be back here in fifteen minutes, about, in case you need more cover."

"Close your eyes, Bernie," Cal said. "It's bright out there."

"I'm not stupid, Calvin Cobble," Berneatha said—then added, reluctantly, "I mean, thanks."

They stepped, again together, into the sunlight, feeling the warmth on their closed eyelids before squinting and—gradually—blinking their eyes open.

They walked close to the red brick building so as not to be seen through the windows above.

When they got to the front door, Cal said, "You wanna do the honors?"

Berneatha turned the knob and nudged the door open a crack. She peered inside, only her eyes and forehead visible to anyone in the cafeteria. "All clear. There's someone in the bathroom, though. I can hear him washing his hands. Better hurry."

"What about Principal Warden? He's not in his office, is he?"

Then there it was: the principal's bellowing from two floors up. Or was it five floors up? It sounded like he was standing right next to them. The two orphans grinned.

"Let's go," Berneatha said.

They speed-walked past the bathroom, where the water was still running—how long was that kid gonna wash his hands?—to Principal Warden's office, where they let themselves in.

Principal Warden's face startled Cal. It was, of course, the nickel bust's red eyes that now stared a hole into Cal's head. He turned and looked at the wall. The dent hadn't been repaired. Perhaps it would stay there forever, a warning to orphans sent to this small and terrifying space to confront their bald and volatile principal. Maybe Principal Warden would write, in magic marker, "Cal Cobble sat here. Where is he now?"

"Let's grab the map and get outta here," Berneatha advised.

They were halfway to the front door—the smell of burnt cheetah-cake and the sound of low chanting evidence that Mr. and Mrs. Grossetta were occupied in the kitchen—when the bathroom door swung open, something wet hit Cal in the back of the head, and they heard a familiar voice.

"Torch?"

Hector Nelson, big and intimidating as ever, the stains below his armpits the brown-yellow color of Dijon mustard, stood in front of the open bathroom door, an inch of water covering the floor and rushing out into the cafeteria.

"Uh, hey, Hector," Cal said, noticing the wad of toilet paper at his feet, the something wet that had hit the back of his head. "What're you doing?"

It took Hector a moment to collect himself. He actually answered Cal's question: "I just came down here to plug up the faucet. See if I could flood the place." Then he regained his composure. He cocked his head, squinted at Cal, looked up to the ceiling, and said, "My prayers have been answered."

To Cal and Berneatha he said, "Say good-bye to your pal, Twiggins. You might not see him again."

Cal was surprised that he wasn't scared. Instead of turning and scrambling up Aunt Robbie's trunk as he had three months before, he eased the brittle newspaper article out of his pocket and stepped toward Hector. "See this?" he said. "This is my dad. Know where he is right now? He's a prisoner at R.I.P. Take a look at the mug shot, huh? See? Ron Cobble. You know where I'm going? To see him. Right now I'm going. You can go take a swim in the bathroom for all I care." He turned to Bernie. "Let's go."

Cal's unexpected aplomb, along with the news he delivered, left Hector frozen and speechless.

As they exited the building, Cal said, "Oh, and Hector?

You tell anyone about this—about me and Bernie being here and where we're going?—I'm going to send my dad after you first."

When they got outside, Mr. Englewood was still all the way down at the rock beach. Berneatha, holding the rolled up map in her right hand, said, "Take a swim in the bathroom, Calvin Cobble? Now that's funny. Didn't really make any sense, though."

"I know. It's just what came out." They stood there until Cal said, "Hey—should we wait for Mr. Englewood against the building, Bernie?"

She looked up into her friend's eyes, admiring his display of self-assurance. "Nah. Race ya back." She took off across the great front lawn, Cal right on her heels.

Chapter 47

That afternoon, three orphans with window seats— one on the third floor, one on the sixth, and one on the seventh—saw a boy with his head on fire and a little girl with clown's feet racing across the lawn toward Mr. E's shack. They didn't believe what they'd seen, though. Must have been another daydream in the middle of another shapeless day at the orphanage at the center of the Earth.

Chapter 48

According to your principal's map," Mr. Englewood said, "we're twenty-three miles from the prison right where we stand. And it's about the same distance from the water as the orphanage is—'bout three-hundred yards is all. So if we follow the shore for twenty-three miles, we'll be one daring dash like that one I just saw out of you two away from our destination."

"Uh, I have a question," said Cal. "How will we know when we've gone twenty-three miles?"

It was Berneatha's turn: "The average person walks three miles an hour. If you slow down, Mr. Englewood, and I speed up, we'll get a pretty good reading of how close we're getting."

"That's awfully wise, Berneatha, but I can do you one better. Should have used this idea earlier, actually, but didn't think of it until you two already tiptoed into the orphanage. I say we take the lawn mower. It's got a clock and even a speedometer. We match one against the other, and we'll always know how far we've gone and how far we need to go. Figure even with two extra passengers, we can get it up to five miles an hour. That means we'll be at that fine penal institution in a little less than five hours. Oh, and one more thing. It's got lights. Don't know they'll do a lot of good in that Shadow, but we'll see what's right in front of us, anyway."

"One more question," Cal said. "Do we have any idea how to get in—you know, how to break into the prison where they keep the evil people and get my dad outta there?"

They looked from one to another.

"Cal, this is your gig," said Mr. Englewood. "You got five hours to come up with a plan."

Chapter 49

Along with themselves, they brought a loaf of bread, a jar of peanut butter, and the map of Robert. They tied a five-gallon jug of gasoline to the back of the seat. All of this was more weight than Mr. Englewood's lawn mower was accustomed to, and its engine's roar now was more a groan. It did its job, though, rolling along the shoreline at a consistent five-mile-per-hour clip. Cal sat on Mr. Englewood's left thigh, Berneatha on his right thigh. His slender legs weren't the most comfortable seats for the two passengers—it was like riding a skinny horse with no saddle—but then this trip wasn't about comfort.

They didn't do much talking. Part of it was the Shadow itself. The coldness of it, the absence of life or energy or light in the air, was unnerving. You were pretty sure no one was around, and yet you still didn't want anyone to hear you. There were vague but very real fears of prisoners roaming the darkness, ears perked, waiting.

The rest of it was Mr. Englewood needing to concentrate. His lawn mower's lights allowed him to see maybe three feet in front of him and no more. The lawn mower rolled along inside a bubble of dim light. Outside the bubble, nothing but black. This made driving in a straight line difficult, and they needed to stay in a straight line for their miles-per-hour to time-of-drive equation to hold. It was all Mr. Englewood could do to keep the lawn mower from veering toward the middle of the island or worse, into Lake Arctic, with its immediate drop-off from the cold dirt shore (there were no skipping stones nor anything resembling a beach in the Shadow) to the deepest body of water in the world. When Mr. Englewood's forearm brushed up against his, Cal felt the sweat and tension brought on by the driver's great effort.

Berneatha occupied herself by leaning forward and staring at the clock and speedometer, calculating their miles traveled and offering periodic whispered updates.

Cal didn't know what to do with himself. He knew he should be coming up with a plan, a way of getting into and then back out of Robert Inner-planet Penitentiary. A way of avoiding highly trained guards and murderously dangerous inmates. But the harder he thought about it, the more paralyzed his brain became. He just couldn't force himself to develop a creative idea.

Instead, Cal drifted away. He lost himself in the darkness, letting his only two friends in the world take care of all immediate concerns. Cal's thoughts drifted to the mother he'd never met. The mother he'd never seen, even in a photograph. The mother he knew had died bringing him to the world, and for what? All so he could live hidden and forgotten in the middle of the planet, twelve years old, often lonely and miserable.

* * *

As Cal thought these thoughts, he wished he could picture his mother. He wondered what it must have been like to be pregnant and have your husband sent to jail. He wondered why all this had happened to her. Was it because of some gene the Cobble males carried? The gene that gave him uncontrollable red-orange hair? The gene that caused his dad to find himself in the deepest of trouble for something he didn't do? Cal and his dad obviously shared the gift of drawing blame for whatever bad happened around them. He'd been in Principal Warden's office more times than he could count. Now there was a dent in the wall where Cal's head used to rest. And here he was, driving Mr. Englewood and Bernie to doom, and he had no idea what would happen next or how to help his dad. If his dad's luck was as bad as his own, how would they ever make it out of the prison?

Cal heard Berneatha, her voice distant, overpowered by the voice narrating his thoughts, say they'd traveled ten miles. Later he heard Mr. Englewood ask if anyone wanted to stop for a sandwich.

They rolled on.

Chapter 50

A crash of glass. One of the lawn mower's lights went out.

Mr. Englewood said, "What the—"

Another crash, and there went the other light.

"Did we just hit something?" Berneatha asked. Mr. Englewood brought the lawn mower to a stop. The darkness was absolute.

They heard footsteps.

"Hey—who's out there!" Berneatha shouted.

In the absolute darkness, they were utterly helpless. They couldn't see one another or even the lawn mower on which they sat. They could only wait and react.

Cal had a thought, a thought whose roots reached deep into hope. "Belinda?" he said, "Belinda Poof? Is that you?"

A man's coarse laugh, more a clearing of the throat than a laugh, dashed Cal's hopes of finding the lost orphan. Cal reached into his pocket and gripped his stone. He couldn't see a target. He didn't even know who or what the target was. But it was better to be ready in some way. And then he and his friends were squinting into a flashlight's beam.

"No. I don't know a Belinda." The man pulled the flashlight's beam back toward him, revealing a dirty, bearded face, the beard long enough Cal couldn't see the ends of it. Cal made out backpack straps on his shoulders. "I'm Bartholomew. Guess people've been calling me Bart for a long time now. Never did like the nickname, though. If you don't mind, you'll all stick with my given name."

* * *

Bartholomew Rogers said, "You're going to want to kill that engine—and keep your voice down, young lady." He kept his flashlight's beam on Cal as he walked around the trio to retrieve the round rocks that had broken the lawn mower's lights. "That is, unless you want every guard and guard dog in Robert on you like flies on a dead deer carcass next to a port-a-potty."

Cal and Berneatha didn't know what to say, and so it was Mr. Englewood who responded first.

"So you the one," Mr. Englewood said. "Mr. Lime Green himself."

Bartholomew half grinned, then shined his flashlight on Mr. Englewood. "And you must be Mr. Herschel Englewood. Heard you were down here." He kept the flashlight on Mr. Englewood a good long time before speaking again. "Let me ask you this, Herschel: Ever wish you could take something back so bad the wish aches in your lower back and runs through your body like contaminated blood?"

"I know that wish," said Mr. Englewood. And Cal thought, *I do, too. Oh, Belinda Poof, I wish I would have screamed*.

"Thought you might," Bartholomew Rogers grunted softly to himself. "Guess there's no better place than the pit of some planet when you feel that way."

"Sounds like we have near the same regret, Bartholomew. Both of us pointing that regret toward the South Pole. Or are we pointing it here, to this place?"

Bartholomew grunted again, turning the flashlight back toward him. "I was sorry to hear about your brother, Herschel."

"I appreciate it. And what about you, Bartholomew. What do you regret?"

Bartholomew dropped his head and peered down to the ground he couldn't see. "Can you believe the celebrity that comes with one unintended discovery? All a man wants is a little money so he can find a few places humans haven't touched. He finds one anomaly, and his country wants him to be a present-day Meriwether Lewis and William Clark. Wants to follow him around with cameras, ask him questions, surround him with people. Wants him to lead them somewhere. Pressures him into writing a book. Everything he spent his life avoiding."

He peered up now, into the darkness.

"Don't know why it took me so long to get down here, to be honest. Guess the thought of it repulsed me. Finding this place—if that's what I did—it ended my career. But you know what, there's not a remoter place than Robert. I've been out here two years now, been the unofficial five hundred and twenty-second resident, and"—now he smiled—"besides guards, you all're the first people I've seen. There are some awfully interesting plant species growing over here. Got to be, to survive in this darkness. Haven't found any animals yet, but I'm looking. If I find anything, I'll make sure not to report it. Last time I reported a discovery, no one would leave me alone for years.

"Anyway—I'll stop blabbing. No offense, but I'm about sick of your company already. I know you didn't come out here to see me, either. I've been all over this island, and there's only one place you could be heading. Heaven knows why you'd want to go there, but I'm sure you have your reasons."

He lifted his backpack off his shoulders, and the light dropped from his face to his hand as he unzipped the pack, fumbled a bit, and removed three tiny flashlights, flipping them on and resting them on the ground. "Take these. Keep the beams low, to the ground. You won't need 'em when you get closer to the building. Just walk to the light."

Bartholomew Rogers walked away, keeping his own beam low. Then he turned and said, "Whatever you do, don't follow me. Ever."

Chapter 51

Careful not to run into one another or the lawn mower, the three walked to the flashlights. They picked the flashlights up, illumined their own faces, and grinned at one another. Mr. Englewood ran his flashlight's beam down his tall body. When the beam returned to his face, he said, "Just making sure all of me was still here. Hadn't seen my legs in awhile."

"Guess we should start walking?" Cal had meant to say it with more confidence.

"We better," Berneatha replied, "unless they're bringing the prison to us instead."

And so they walked, their beams aimed at the ground a couple feet in front of them and no more, doing as America's great explorer, the man who had spent two years in the Shadow, had instructed. The flashlights weren't powerful, but they did keep the three together and walking in a generally straight direction.

"How far you think we need to walk?" Cal asked.

"Bartholomew made it sound like we'd see it real soon," answered Mr. Englewood.

And then there it was.

First it was a hazy light in the offing—far, far ahead of them, it seemed, and expanding as they moved toward it. "Suppose this is when we turn off our flashlights, gang," said Mr. Englewood. "Just walk to the light."

They hooked elbows and moved toward the hazy light.

When they were several hundred yards out from the prison, they knew their flashlights would be of no use to them the rest of the way. They would never want for light once they stepped into the prison's glow. Cal, Mr. Englewood, and Berneatha tucked the flashlights in their pockets for later—whatever and whenever that meant.

The horseshoe-shaped, cement-walled Robert Innerplanet Penitentiary glowed like a night-light. Eleven stories high and half a mile from one end of the horseshoe around to the other, it was an impressive structure. They couldn't see any guards, but they must have been somewhere near.

This was the closest thing to sunlight the troupe had seen in hours, and yet it wasn't comforting.

They had stopped near a light tower, one of the countless that surrounded the prison campus. Berneatha leaned as if she were going to rest her weight against the tower, then thought better of it. "The prisoners. They can't see us because we're in the dark, right?"

"That's what I'm thinking, Berneatha," Mr. Englewood said. "You too young to remember what it's like to have the light on in your bedroom? You keep it on, and the world out in the street, it can see you. You turn off the bedroom light, you can see the world."

"That makes sense. But how in the world are we gonna sneak in there?"

Staring up at the prison, the structure ghostly in the Shadow's dark, Mr. Englewood looked deep in thought. His eyes moved to the light tower, from its base all the way up to the vertical rectangle that held hundreds of light bulbs. "Looks kinda like a toothbrush, doesn't it?" he said to himself. Then he brought his eyes back down. "You got a plan yet, Cal?"

Cal closed his eyes and breathed deeply, steeling himself. What he had in mind wasn't going to be easy. He wasn't sure he wanted to get his friends tangled up in it. And yet they'd come this far for him, hadn't they?

"Yeah," he said. "I think I do."

Chapter 52

Y ou two ready? Soon as we step into that light, they'll be on us like them flies Bartholomew mentioned."

Berneatha looked at her friend. "You need to do this, right, Calvin Cobble?"

"Yeah, Bernie, I really think I do."

She took a deep breath and said, "Then let's move, Mr. Englewood."

Mr. Englewood, his hands on their backs, gently pushed them into Robert Inner-planet Penitentiary's glow.

On cue, so fast it was almost surreal, eight guards dressed in navy blue emerged (from where?) and surrounded them, their rifles pointed. A siren howled. A voice boomed: "Take the next step, and you won't take another."

They were cuffed and pushed through the mall to the door in the middle of the horseshoe-shaped building. As it turned out, it was five doors. The guard unlocked the first door with an old-fashioned house key. The next he unlocked with a key card. The third door he unlocked by punching in a number code. Three guards turned Cal, Mr. Englewood, and Berneatha around so they couldn't watch him punch in the number. The next door the guard unlocked with a thumb print. And to unlock the fifth and final door into the prison, the guard pushed a button, and a man appeared on a small television screen. "Warden, we have three trespassers here, two of them minors. They walked onto the campus"—he looked at his watch—"two hundred and thirteen seconds ago."

The warden squinted, thinking. "Bring them up here, Mr. Jefferson. I'll want to talk with them." There was a buzz, and they could hear the door automatically unlock. The guard pulled it open. And then they were in.

* * *

A staircase, straight and narrow and steeper than steep.

That was the first thing Cal noticed as he entered the prison. Really, that's all there was to notice at first glance. The bottom floor all around the horseshoe was empty. Just a concrete floor and concrete walls that rose fifty feet before meeting the first rusty iron grill walkway.

Cells, with what must have been bullet-proof glass in front of them, lined the grill walkway. The cells were lit by halogen tubes running all the way down the ceiling of each horseshoe leg. Spotlights came from small structures attached to the walkway fence, one light in front of each cell, removing any chance of shadow from the cells. There were ten identical floors of cells in each wing of the horseshoe. Short, rusty staircases connected one grill walkway to the next, all the way up to the tenth floor. The staircases were never on top of one another, however; if you walked up the short staircase from the first floor of cells to the second, you'd have to walk fifty paces to get to another staircase. If an inmate were to somehow escape his cell—how that would be possible was anyone's guess—the inmate would never have a straight shot to the floor, Cal figured; he'd have to zigzag around his wing to get to the lowest grill walkway, and then he was still fifty feet above the five doors, each locked in a different manner.

There were two hundred inmates, each with his or her own cell. Cal could see them plainly from where he stood. Each sat in a chair in the middle of the cell. They wore black straightjackets that contrasted the building's bright lights. None of the cells had windows.

And then a prisoner in a straightjacket appeared, walking down the horseshoe leg to their left. As he passed one inmate's cell, the inmate inside his cell looked up, apparently ready to say something. And then the voice Cal, Mr. Englewood, and Berneatha had heard as they stepped into R.I.P.'s light—the warden's voice, Cal now realized—boomed again: "Mr. Studer, eyes to the floor. Let Mr. Oakley finish his daily exercise in peace." The inmate in the cell looked back down, the exercising inmate continuing his walk as if nothing had happened.

Was Cal's dad really one of them? Was he here?

The guards pushed Cal, Mr. Englewood, and Berneatha in single-file up the steep staircase in front of them.

At the top of the staircase was a short cement floor at the center of the horseshoe. The floor was between the fifth and sixth floors of cells, vertically, though it didn't extend all the way over to them. There were staircases attached to each wing that a person could take from the short floor in the middle of the facility down to the fifth floor of cells and up to the sixth floor of cells. A guard had access to the cells only through this short floor in the middle of the horseshoe and then, as a prisoner would, had to zigzag down or up to whatever floor he patrolled that morning, day, or night.

In the middle of this short floor was a wooden door, the words Warden's Office, Robert Inner-planet Penitentiary embossed in gold on the door. Before the guard in front of Cal knocked on the office door, the warden's voice came through: "It's unlocked, Jefferson."

The guard opened the door, ushered the trespassers through, and popped his head in to hear the warden say, "That will be all, Mr. Jefferson. I'll deal with them from here," and took his leave.

The door closed behind them, and it was just the two orphans, the lawn mower, and the warden in the room. Except they weren't alone. Miniature television screens covered the back wall, each one featuring a different cell. The warden could keep an eye on all two hundred prisoners at once.

"I assume you know where you are," the warden said, his back to them as he watched the screens above him. "So the question, of course"—he turned to face them, a middle-aged man with a pointy nose, Wall Street hair, and an athletic build wearing a sharp gray suit—"is why you're here. Mr. Englewood, the adult in the room—why don't you begin." The warden brandished three pieces of paper, each with a picture of Cal, Mr. Englewood, or Berneatha. Underneath the photographs were their names, their ages, and their roles on the island. Cal's read:

Calvin Comet Cobble, 12
Orphan, Hidden Shores Orphanage

Mr. Englewood said, "Warden, I saw these two running off into the Shadow. Don't tell me why they'd do a thing like that. I ask the principal, back at the orphanage, and he tells me he doesn't know, either, but would I please go retrieve them. By the time I caught up to them, I could see this place up in front of us, and I figured the principal would want a phone call. I figured he'd want to know where his students were and sooner than I could get them back to him. Trip takes half a day, walking."

"Uh-huh. So you three are all the way out here because these two decided to run away." He walked in front of his desk. "They must have had a reason to come out here. Mr. Cobble," he tapped the last name on the piece of paper, perhaps pausing for just a moment, "let's start with you."

"Me?" Cal had been busy. He'd been battling nerves, like the other two, but he'd also been trying to find his dad on the miniature television screens. He hadn't found him up there yet, and if his dad wasn't here, if he wasn't a prisoner at R.I.P., then he didn't know anything anymore. He certainly didn't know how his plan would work. "I, uh, I live at Hidden Shores—"

"This part I know, Mr. Cobble."

"Right. I mean, well, I found out that my dad—Ron Cobble?—that he might be here. I've never met my parents, and I, well, I needed to see my dad, so I ran out here."

"And I certainly wasn't going to let him come out here all on his own," Berneatha said, not to be left out of the conversation.

"Right. Yeah, Bernie followed me out here, and I let her tag along."

"You let me? I was doing you a favor."

"It doesn't matter, Bernie."

"It doesn't matter to *you*, Calvin Cobble."

"Enough," the warden said. "So you ran out here. And just how did you intend to see your dad?"

"Well, honestly, I had no idea. I just, well, I knew I had to see him, you know?"

"No. I don't know, Mr. Cobble. This is not a place you just show up at, hoping to see someone. Do you understand that?"

"Yeah. I mean, yes, I know, I just—but is he here? My dad?"

"That is the least of your concerns, Mr. Cobble," the warden said, and Berneatha elbowed Cal and whispered, "That means he's here." The warden continued: "And, Mr. Englewood—you should know better than to bring these orphans here. Next time—not that there will ever be a next time, you two; this half of the island is a dangerous place—turn them back around and take them home.

"Make your phone call brief. Then my guards will escort you off the premises."

Mr. Englewood went to the phone, picked it up, and dialed. After a short wait, he said, "Sir, this is Herschel Englewood."

And then Cal turned, scrambled through the open door, and ran across the short floor and up the stairs leading to one wing of the horseshoe's sixth floor. The floor clanged each time he stomped on it.

The warden stepped out the door and yelled, "Son! What do you think you're going to accomplish?"

Cal replied, "I'm going to see my dad," as Berneatha quietly closed and locked the office door behind the warden.

Cal ran. He ducked down one short staircase in front of a guard, reversed direction, and made it to another staircase before the guard on the next floor reached him. He sprinted down the stairs, each step producing a metallic thud. Three times he looked over and saw the prisoners at his side, evil in their eyes, standing up and howling as he ran. Fear crawled up his spine, but he ignored it and kept running. Six years at an orphanage next to the darkest Shadow in the world, and he could handle fear. He peered into their cells as he ran, hoping. He needed to see his dad. He needed to help him.

And then he went down one more staircase, and a guard met him there, wrapping him up so tight in his arms Cal thought the man might have cobras under his shirt. With no hope of escape from the man's strong arms, Cal took a deep breath. He knew his search for his dad was over.

The guard picked him up, crushing Cal's knees into his chest. "That was the dumbest thing you've ever done, kid." He carried Cal back up three sets of staircases and over to the warden's short floor. He set Cal down on his knees, pivoted, and returned to duty on his floor. The guards had now returned to walking their floors and were ordering prisoners back to their chairs. All around him, Cal heard the decrescendo of the inmates' howls, and then everything was quiet again.

The warden looked down at Cal and said. "This, too, son, will have to be reported to your principal. I encourage you to feel relieved that only his name is Warden and not his occupation."

Cal heard Berneatha's laugh from inside the office. "I wouldn't be so sure of that," she said.

The warden turned to open his office door and then couldn't. The doorknob wouldn't rotate. He sighed and said through the door in a voice level and scary, "Miss Twiggins, open this door. Now. I will not ask again."

When it didn't open, the warden looked to the guard

on the sixth floor. "Mr. Peterson—would you lend me a hand?"

The guard made his way down the stairs. When he joined them on the short floor, he lowered his shoulder, bent his knees, and heaved himself into the warden's door, busting the lock and throwing the door wide open.

The warden stepped into the room as Mr. Englewood held up the phone and said, "Warden. It's for you."

Chapter 53

The warden had kicked them out of his office, and so Cal and Mr. Englewood stood outside it with Berneatha between them. Two guards were there, too, one on either side of them. Cal looked Mr. Englewood in the eyes and said, "Thank you."

"It's what we came to do, Cal. Let's hope it all works out. The President said he'd look into it, make sure your dad would get another trial. Said he'd dig up all the newspapers I told him about and take a look at your dad's record prior to the bank robbery. He'll have a good shot at getting off."

Cal nodded. "Then that's all we can do, right?"

"Yeah, Cal. We done a lot."

Cal nodded again. "Hey, you too, Bernie. Thanks."

"Yeah, yeah. Thanks for letting me *tag along*."

She pushed Cal, and he bumped her back.

The warden reappeared then and said to one of the

guards, "Please escort the young man to cell A910."

The guard stammered. "Sir. That's—you don't mean Cobble's cell? He hasn't spoken, hasn't said a word in years."

"Yes, Mr. Becker, that is the cell I mean. When you get there, the boy gets 90 seconds alone."

"Alone in the cell, sir?"

"Alone in the cell, Mr. Becker."

* * *

Getting up to the ninth floor at their deliberate pace took several minutes—up one staircase and over, up another staircase and over again, three times. On the ninth floor, the guard led Cal to the last cell on the right. As they approached, the guard said into his radio, "We're here, sir."

"Yes. I see that, Mr. Becker," the warden's voice replied. And then the bullet-proof glass rose twenty-seven inches, and the guard said, "Cobble, you have a visitor."

Ron Cobble was a small, round-shouldered man. Most of the prisoners made the plastic chairs on which they sat look tiny, as if they were kid chairs that came in a play tea party set, but Ron sat comfortably in his. The way he curled his legs under the chair, it seemed as if his legs were barely long enough to touch the ground. Tufts of thinning red-orange hair sprung from the top of his head.

"Slide on in there, son. Good luck."

Cal got down on his stomach and slithered under

the glass. As soon as he was on the other side, the glass descended again to the floor.

He stood up, inches from his father. Cal looked into his father's pale face. He watched his father's unseeing eyes, fixated on the floor. "Um—Dad? It's me, Calvin."

His dad didn't respond. "Can you hear me, Dad? Dad, you're going to get another trial—my friend, Mr. Englewood, he arranged it. I mean, I know you didn't do it, Dad, so you'll get off, I know it. And then maybe, maybe I can come live with you."

Ron Cobble sat in the chair, unresponsive, his eyes still glued to the floor of his cell. Cal didn't know what else to say. He hadn't seen his dad before, not in his whole life. He'd never talked with him about a single subject, and now it felt as if Cal had nothing left to tell the man. The questions he'd always wanted answered—Where was his dad? Why had he abandoned Cal and his mom?—had already been answered. Cal hadn't been abandoned; his dad had been sent to the most secure prison in the world. The man had suffered, Cal was sure, more in one day than Cal had in seven years at Robert. All of this time, they'd lived in the same forgotten city, and neither of them knew it. He felt the tears welling up inside him, as they had that day on the beach with Mr. Englewood.

He heard the warden's voice: "Young Mr. Cobble, your time is nearly up. The glass behind you will rise in a moment. Please exit as you entered."

Cal looked up one more time at his dad, wanting to see him again and yet not knowing if this was the image he wanted of his father, frail and removed from the world.

"Dad!" he screamed. "I'm Calvin Comet Cobble, your—"

"Daughter." Ron wheezed the word, looking up at Cal for the first time.

Cal stood there, confused. "No, Dad. I'm your son. You mean son, right?"

Ron nodded his head slowly, his eyes tearing up. Cal stepped closer, and Ron began to cry. He leaned his forehead against Cal's chest. "Yes. Son. I mean son," he whispered. "You—you know what I mean. My son knows what I mean." And then Ron Cobble looked up into Cal's face, his eyes clear and intense. "I've endured for you, son."

The guard's voice behind Cal: "Time's up, kid."

Cal put his hand on his dad's shoulder, leaned forward, and kissed his forehead. "We're going to do everything we can, Dad. Everything we can to get you out of here."

And then Cal thought of something. He reached into his pocket and found his stone. "Dad," he said. "This is for you—a present."

Ron Cobble watched the white, gray-splotched stone in his son's hand. He smiled a small smile and said, "Beautiful moonrise tonight, don't you think? You keep it, son. Your mother would want you to have it."

Chapter 54

With their flashlights aimed high, they found the riding lawn mower in no time.

And then they headed home.

Mr. Englewood drove, of course, as Cal and Berneatha sat on his knees and held up their flashlights in place of the lights Bartholomew Rogers shattered hours earlier. The driving was easier on the way home. It always is. On the way home, you know where you're going. Mr. Englewood felt free to veer into the middle of the island now that they weren't hiding from anyone or keeping track of their miles traveled.

As on the way to the prison, they didn't talk much. They had accomplished what they'd set out to accomplish, and that was enough.

Chapter 55

When they got back to Mr. Englewood's shack, it was early in the morning. Sunlight crept through the hole in the Mantle. Berneatha fell asleep immediately on top of six stacks of newspapers.

Standing in the shack, Cal said, "I know I already said it, Mr. Englewood—but thanks. I mean, I never would have seen my dad without you."

"No need to thank me. I mean it. I think that Bartholomew Rogers, he's on to something. This life, it's all about finding where you belong, why you're here. A long time ago, I did something selfish. Paid the price, too. No, Cal, I think most of us are here to help one another. At least help the ones who mean something to us. You gave me a chance to do that."

Cal liked what Mr. Englewood said about being here to help the people you care about. Agreeing but not knowing how to respond, he asked, "Do you—do you wanna skip stones this morning?"

Mr. Englewood smiled down at Cal with his eyes. "You know, Cal Cobble, I think I'm going to sit this one out and close my eyes for a few hours. I think you got something to do on your own, anyway."

* * *

Cal walked over the purplish rocks, knowing for the first time in his twelve years on and inside the planet that everything would be okay. He and Berneatha would help each other get through the next two and a half years at Hidden Shores. They could handle Miss Trudy, Hector Nelson, and even Principal Warden. Cal would spend every morning with Mr. Englewood. His dad would get his trial. With Cal's help, Mr. Englewood's, Berneatha's, and even the former President's—Cal's dad might be set free and returned to the outside world.

Maybe his dad would be his legal guardian and Berneatha's, too. Maybe Mr. Englewood would return with them to the surface. Maybe. For now, Cal would concentrate on living here, in Robert, at the center of the world. It was just a place, even a home, as was any other.

Where he lived? It was, indeed, out of his control. *How* he felt and how he lived? He got to decide those things. And Belinda Poof? He probably could have stopped her; he knew that. He could have yelled. He could have run into the Shadow and grabbed her and at least made sure she wasn't alone. No, not *could* have. *Should* have. He should have helped her. It hurt Cal to admit it, but doing so gave him strength. It gave him control.

Cal took his stone out of his right front pocket. He looked it over once more, admiring its resemblance to the moon, that thing way out there, that had drawn him to the window to see Mr. Englewood skip a stone for the first time. And then he moved closer to the water. He dug his feet in, moved his weight over to his back foot, pushed off, and threw the stone submarine-style as far and as close to the water as he could. It hit the beam of sunlight and bounded forward—again and again and again. It skipped twenty-seven times before dropping under the surface. His best skip yet.

Cal looked out at the water and watched the rings caused by his stone expand and get swallowed up by the great calm lake. He watched with a sense of satisfaction and little sadness.

After all, he could always skip another stone tomorrow.

Loose Ends

So where did Belinda Poof go, you ask? You already know. She disappeared. She walked into a deep dark Shadow never to be seen again.

Perhaps you find that depressing. You should. A scary place stole from the world a decent person.

But take some solace, reader.

Somewhere in Detroit, the morning after a night of heavy rain, an earthworm made it safely across a busy street to live another day. To one boy, that earthworm made all the difference.

Discussion Questions

1. In *Skipping Stones at the Center of the Earth*, characters are affected by a discovery in many ways. Can you think of a major event in your life, at your school, or in history that impacted a great variety of people in different ways? Which people did this event affect, and how so?

2. Cal Cobble is discriminated against because of the color of his hair and because of what people believe his dad did. Do you know anyone who is treated a certain way because of how they look or whom they're related to?

3. While *Skipping Stones* tells the stories of several characters, it focuses on Cal Cobble. How would the book be different if it focused on another character? Mr. Englewood, perhaps, or Bartholomew Rogers?

4. We learn early in the book that Robert is a place that has been forgotten about, and that means its citizens have been forgotten about, too. Mr. Englewood tells Cal that people don't want to think about a place as terrible as Robert. Are there places near you or around the world that people seem to have forgotten about? Why don't people want to think about those places?

5. At an exciting point in *Skipping Stones*, the narrator says that "and then" are a storyteller's favorite words. Do you think the narrator's right? What is meant by this?

6. Does *Skipping Stones at the Center of the Earth* remind you of any other books you've read? Which ones? How so?

7. According to Mr. Englewood, you shouldn't skip stones "until you're old enough to be silent for a time." Why? What does he mean by this? Can you relate?

8. Hueller's story asks readers to suspend their disbelief—to imagine a made-up place and indulge in fantastical events. Like any good yarn, however, it's not all make-believe. Are there any facts or truths presented in the book that surprised you?

About the Author

Andy Hueller is the author of *Dizzy Fantastic and Her Flying Bicycle*. He teaches at St. Paul Academy and Summit School and lives in Minneapolis with his wife, Debbie. He gives Cal Cobble credit for leading him to a career writing for younger readers. "I closed my eyes one day years ago and saw this boy with flaming red-orange hair and freckles that looked like smoldering embers. For some reason, he was living in a remote place and didn't have many friends. I wanted to figure out why he lived so far away and what it was like to be picked on for reasons he couldn't control."

Learn more about Andy, Cal, and of course Dizzy at www.andrewhueller.com.

Do you want to learn more about Robert, AK? Do you have some insight regarding the whereabouts of Belinda Poof? Check out http://whateverhappenedtobelindapoof.blogspot.com.

0 26575 54884 6